I0456835

PARADISE SYMPHONY

A NOIR HORROR THRILLER

ALEXANDER SEMENYUK

This is a work of fiction. Names, characters, places, and incidents are products of the author's imagination or are used fictitiously and are not to be construed as real. Any resemblance to actual events, locations, organizations, or persons, living or dead, is entirely coincidental.

World Castle Publishing, LLC
Pensacola, Florida
Copyright © Alexander Semenyuk 2022
Hardback ISBN: 9798359835824
Paperback ISBN: 9781958336779
eBook ISBN: 9781958336786
First Edition World Castle Publishing, LLC, December 5, 2022
http://www.worldcastlepublishing.com
Licensing Notes
Cover: Igor Olszewski
Editor: Maxine Bringenberg

CHAPTER ONE

I was no longer a man who could run quickly, move hastily, or maneuver with great dexterity. Despite this, I was still good at my job — in fact, perhaps even better than ever — but I rarely took up any cases anymore. Retirement was on my mind, as my son was now a man and was off studying at a university. However, life always had major surprises in store for me, and when I was offered a particular case, something deep inside me began to burn once again. My wife, Ida, opposed this, but the case drew me to it in a powerful way.

I am Luc Nistage, and this is a journal of my one final case — perhaps the most terrifying yet.

One day as I had my morning coffee with Ida and went out to grab the latest newspaper,

a young man came running. He was excited
and relieved to see me. He had a big forehead,
small eyes, and large, horselike teeth. Bless his
heart. What an ugly creature.

"Mr. Nistage? I've been looking all over
for you!"

"Really? And why? Who may you be?"

Luckily there was a small café with
outdoor tables near our townhome, and I sat
down at one of them with the young man.

"My name is Thompson Larsson.
Through my father's investment in our case,
I was able to find a lead, which brought me
to you. Someone who has experience in such
matters."

"What matters?"

The boy's brow furrowed. "Missing
people...strange occurrences, cults."

A sigh escaped my lips. "I'm not sure I'm
up to a case like that, young lad."

"Have you heard of the book titled
Agghtthg Isakolm?"

For some reason, this name sent chills
down my spine as an image of an old tentacled

adversary from the ocean flashed in my mind.

Still, "I don't think so. What is it?"

The boy drank from his water glass. "From what I have learned, it means "Deep Symphony." He stopped to drink again. "It's a book my sister Natalie heard about from a man in her book club. He suggested it to the members. We thought nothing of it, but that was before she went missing, along with everyone else in the club. She left behind drawings, writings, a journal — with many strange things."

He took out a large package of papers and a journal wrapped in paper and string and gave them to me.

His eyes pleaded with me. "All I ask is that you look over these and then tomorrow let me know if you'll help me. I will pray that you do."

After getting my newspaper and parting with the young man, I went back to our place. Ida had left a note saying she had gone to the store. I set the package of papers and the journal on my desk, opened them, and began to read and observe the images.

The more I read the girl's journal, the more familiar the sinister atmosphere around it became. Then I saw her drawings. They were of weird creatures of various shapes and sizes, including a tall humanoid creature with six tentacles. It said "Aggtthog," but that was also written on all the other drawings. What could it mean? More so, "Aggtthog" was referred to in her strange writings in several places. The man who seemed to be the person who had introduced her to these ideas was named Mijec. Another man she mentioned was Tom Pritt, a friend, I supposed. Those were the only leads. Of course, I was intrigued.

When Ida came back, I told her of the proposition. She sank into her chair.

"Have you lost your mind? You were going to finally retire. You haven't taken a case like this in decades!" Ida threw her hands up in the air.

"Actually, none since I met you, and only one like it before that. But this poor young man and his family are suffering."

Ida looked stern. "Millions of people

suffer each day. Your place is here with your family."

This was going to be a hard sell to my wife. "I realize that, but please, let me look into it. I promise I'll be careful, nothing extreme!"

Ida got up and flounced out of the room. Of course, she did not really want to listen; she was frightened and angry with me, and she was right, it was a crazy thing to do. Yet I called the young man and arranged a meeting with him the following day.

CHAPTER TWO

It was midday when I met this unfortunate young man at a café called Calgun's. I bought him a beer and began our discussion.

"What can you tell me about the man named Mije?"

The boy looked annoyed, pressing his lips together over his large teeth. "She described him to me a few times, but I never met him. She said he was bald, tall, middle-aged."

"What else do you know about him?"

The boy's look was earnest. "I asked everyone she knew, but all the members of this club vanished, and her other friends had no idea. They'd never met him."

I sat back in my chair. "Did the club always meet in the same place?"

"No." Thompson shook his head.

"Although they met at some places more than once."

"Such as?" I prompted.

"The Double Trouble piano café and the Shaman Alley night club."

"Book readings and meetings in such places?" This struck me as odd. Most book groups met in libraries, bookstores, or coffee shops.

"My sister said they had meeting rooms somewhere there."

I decided to be direct. "What does Aggtthog mean to you?"

His face grew pale, and his hands noticeably shook, and he began to sweat a little. Thompson drew his sleeve across his forehead and took a long pull on his bottle of beer. "At first, I thought she was having mental issues, you know? Talking about some awful creature. But then, one night, I started to have strange dreams. He began to speak to me, calling out to me.

"I had visions of dark waters, waves, some sort of a large building and a lighthouse by the cliffs...." He wiped his brow again. "I don't understand it, but I went to the doctor, and he prescribed me a strong medication that helps me not to have any dreams. But sometimes, it still breaks through, and I still see the visions and hear him.

"In the visions, I see his shape, just like she drew him. It's almost a human, but with six tentacles and scaly skin, and the eyes! I don't know how to describe them...no such color exists in our world." Thompson was clearly shaken, and I felt sorry for the boy.

"Okay," I said as soothingly as I could. "Calm down, young man. That's enough information. You can go home. I assume you know of my rates already?"

"My father will pay double."

"That is not necessary, but if he insists, I will put it away for my son's future." I stood up and extended my hand to him. "I will take your case." (*And Ida will have my hide*, I thought.)

"Thank you so much!" The boy jumped up, took my hand, and pumped it up and down several times.

The look of relief and happiness greatly improved Thompson's looks, and with a radiant smile, he rushed out of the café and down the street. I took a more leisurely pace.

This case must not get Ida or my son Mark involved in any way. I knew I had to tread very carefully. At the same time, I could feel a familiar old rush of excitement and my brain began to work busily. My first target would be that Double Trouble piano café.

I took the rest of the day to make notes and do some research. I went to bed early. Ida elected to stay up. She wasn't speaking to me much in her disapproval.

It had been many years since I'd had a nightmare about creatures from the deep, but this night they came back.

I was sitting on a bench overlooking a large, beautiful, old-style resort, the kind with waiters in bow ties, tennis courts, and beach cabanas. Next to it stood an old white and red lighthouse. The waves were calm. Then in front of me materialized an almost transparent figure, but I could see the outlines of the tentacles in the air. It spoke in a deep voice.

"You are now ready to embrace the knowledge of the deep with the horrors of your past. You misunderstood them. Your mind must open and expand now. We are ready to welcome you." I tried to cry out, but my throat seemed to be closed, and I could not make a sound.

"Find the book!" the creature went on. "You must kill our other servant and prove to us you deserve to be part of our eternal rule over the deep waters. Listen to our deep symphony!"

Then everything turned into a color I could not describe; it was nothing that I had a word for. I felt my pupils expand. Then a wild and powerful sound came from all around me. It seemed to drill deep into my head. I fell to my knees and began to scream in pain. My head felt like it was going to explode.

"Transformation! Transform!" yelled the voice.

I woke up with Ida shaking me. I sat up quickly. I was sweating, and my body was trembling.

She shook her head at me. "You are too old to take on such things, don't you understand?"

Her eyes were filled with sorrow. Why couldn't I just decide to drop this case now? But I couldn't. I felt compelled to solve this mystery.

The next morning I sat at the table, drinking a large cup of coffee and reading a newspaper. Sad, soul-crushing things were happening around the world and in our country. It seemed as though there were endless wars. I thought about what wars could do to men. I had met a few of those. War was a brutal business, where the young died while the old politicians just got richer. I was glad I had kept my son away from it all. It took a lot of convincing. Now he wanted to be a private investigator after university. Well, as long as he had no cases like my newest one, then that path was at least better than war. I flipped through the pages and found some local news. Nothing was cheerful. Why not? There were so many good things happening also, but that was not the business these writers were in. Oh well. I threw the newspaper aside and thought about my dream.

Ida was on the couch, reading a book and sipping her tea. She was even more upset with me. I wished she could see the situation as I did.

I finished my coffee and took out a city map. I traced a route to the university where the girl Natalie had attended and decided to pay a visit there first. Then I wanted to see how convenient it would be to get from there to the Double Trouble.

Travel was much easier these days. I still remembered my older cases — getting around town required a lot of walking, which had taken precious time. Today the cars were fast, and there were taxicabs everywhere. I hailed one and got inside. The middle-aged Slavic immigrant, Vova, was often our driver since we did not own a car.

"Where to, Mister Luc?"

"Smithon University, please."

"Got studying to catch up, hahaha!"

I liked Vova's attitude. He was always upbeat and making jokes. Vova must have had to work nearly about sixty hours a week to provide for his family. I always left a good tip.

The city streets were quick to fill up. People were rushing to their jobs or impatient to do some shopping. The world had changed; things were so much more hectic. Yet Ida and I had been able to find peace during all these years together, to raise a son, and overcome all the obstacles we faced.

The changes in the world had many positives as well, although some days I found it hard to see many of them. As I gazed out the cab's window, lost in my thoughts, we passed by the beautiful Church of St. Therese. I often went there in the evening to pray. Seeing it brought a smile to my face. A traffic jam slowed us down considerably, but not enough to bother me.

"How are the kids, Vova?"

"Very good, good. Growing fast! Soon they can work too! Hahaha, at least one will!"

"That is good. I'm glad to hear that things

seem to be going well for you."

Vova grinned into the rear view mirror, showing his gold front tooth. "Of course, my friend!"

Finally, we arrived at the university. I asked Vova to keep the meter running and wait for me and slipped him some cash. He gladly agreed, and I was on my way. This campus was large, but I had a good idea of where to start.

I went straight to the school's massive library building. It was built in an old Greek style with lovely fluted marble columns at the entrance. Inside I approached the desk, and an older gentleman with an elegant head and a tired look greeted me. I asked him if I could look at the past events and readings schedule. Although he was a bit cranky, he assisted me well, and soon I was sitting at a table, looking through the pages.

Half an hour went by, and I got myself a coffee. I kept on combing through the notices.

"Agghtthog Isakolm."

I finally found it. There was one event by this name. He had come here, as I suspected. I wondered how many people he had entrapped and enchanted besides Natalie, Mark's sister. I found only this one mention of it, so clearly, he was careful, this Mije.

I approached the older gentleman again and asked him about the event. "I have no recollection of it," he said as he peered through his spectacles at the paper I showed him.

Discouraged, I slouched back to the table. Was this all I could extract here?

"The Oracle of the Ancients."

I heard a pleasant female voice and turned my head. A young woman with short black hair and a pale face sat down at the table with me. She looked like a student.

"I beg your pardon?"

The girl smiled. "The Oracle of the Ancients. You were asking about it, about the book. Aggtthog is his other name."

Chills ran down my spine as she said the name.

"How do you know about this?"

"I was there for that reading. Afterwards, everyone went out with the speaker. I was going to as well, but I was notified about a family emergency and went home. Later, in the following days and weeks, a few others nagged me to come to more readings in other locations, but I did not feel good about it. I kept hearing him in my head, the voice...I still do." She smiled a bit sheepishly, then looked concerned. "The others all disappeared eventually. I wonder if I should have gone too, to get rid of the voice...."

"What does he tell you?"

She thought for a moment. "About a town at the ocean, about becoming one with the waters, about learning their 'truth.'" She shrugged. "I just think whoever they are, they must feed on our energy."

I wasn't happy hearing this. "I fear you are right. They also feed on memories and fears. By the way, I am detective Luc Nistage."

The girl smiled and shook my hand. "My name is Sinki. I hope you can find out what is going on and stop the voice. That's all I know — sorry I can't tell you more."

"That was plenty; here is my information,

Sinki," I said, handing her my card. "If you ever feel alone in this, call me. I'll be glad to talk. I will do my best to get to the bottom of it."

She responded, "Just not the bottom of the ocean."

I wasn't sure if she had made a bad joke or if she was serious, as the expression on her pale face remained unchanged. I nodded and left the library. Vova was waiting, and I was ready to visit Double Trouble.

CHAPTER THREE

The part of the city where the nightclub was had narrow and dark streets even during daylight, as the buildings were tall, with retail stores and restaurants on the ground floor. I felt a mix of emotions. This stuff still scared me, but it also made me curious. I still had that spark in me, the craving to do something good.

Vova parked his cab in front of a skyscraper. A neon sign over a red door at the street level proclaimed "Double Trouble Piano Bar."

As I entered, there was a small lobby with red walls and a hallway leading off each side of it. No one was there to greet me. I waited patiently. To my right, I noticed a framed poem on the wall. I went closer to it.

The poem was titled, "The Fire of the

Dragon Phoenix." I proceeded to read it:

"Silence fell upon the lands,
Long it's been since the sky rang
Bells of fury, which shook thy hands,
Bards rejoiced and songs they sang.

Simple men forgot the rules,
The cycle of life, constant refreshing
They ignored the rebirth, silly fools,
The Dragon Phoenix has his blessing.

Once again the sky felt thunder
Of the wings which do not shatter,
Fire spread in deadly wonder
They remembered things that matter.

From the ashes they must rise
As the Dragon Phoenix did,
When with fire the old world dies,
A new existence opens up its lid."

"Ah, that poem, it's a metaphor for
something only a few know about. But

nevertheless, even if you don't, it's a nice poem. My name is Tom Pritt."

A short, rather tubby man in a flamboyant yellow suit with a raspy voice, small eyes, a short beard, and long hair stretched out his hand to me. I shook it—he had clammy hands and a weak grip. I had a bad feeling about the place.

"What brings you here, Mr...?"

"Luc Nistage. I'm a private detective, but also a fan of old music. I understand I might hear something to remind me of past times here?"

The little man chortled. "Of course, of course! Come on in, relax, have a drink, listen, enjoy our girls. The cover charge is twenty dollars, but today be my guest and enter free of charge."

"Thank you, Tom."

I proceeded inside, beyond another red door. I entered a large room with dim lights, dark wood tables, and comfortable chairs. The walls were red, and the floor was black. At the far end was a stage, which was also barely lit.

Tom pointed at a small table for me.

"The next performance is in fifteen minutes. You're in luck. The Collette twins will be performing today."

He left, and I was alone at the table. I looked around and noticed several couples and a few solitary patrons. Even thought it was midday, the place was almost full. I wondered what went on in the rooms down the halls leading off the reception area. Most likely, there were restrooms and a coatroom, and Pritt's office, but perhaps there were rooms for other entertainments.

A lovely waitress in red approached and offered the drinks menu to me, but I ordered black tea. She smiled and left, and a few minutes later, she was back with a hot cup of black tea.

I was sipping slowly and looking around, examining the place. There was no way they did readings in this room. Which hall should I check first? I continued to sip on tea. The best thing was to wait for the music to start. Then I could look around while people were distracted by the entertainment.

The lights dimmed even more, and two petite women took the stage and sat at a pair of baby grand pianos opposite each other. They were indeed identical twins with Continental European features. The moment they began playing a slow melody and humming to it in synch with each other, the whole place became still, as if everyone were on edge. Then they began to sing a slow, beautiful song in French. I had no idea what the words meant, but the sound was mesmerizing. I snapped out of it and quietly made my way to the reception area and down the hallway leading off the right side of the room.

The long hallway was mostly dark, with just a few sconces with red lights on the walls. A sign near the end of the hall said, "Restrooms." There was a ladies' room on one side and a men's room on the other. Next to the restroom was an unmarked black door. I looked farther down the hall and thought I saw a shadow move, so I entered the restroom. It was illuminated brighter than the rest of the place, well-appointed with silver and black geometric wallpaper, and exceptionally clean. I splashed a little bit of cold water on my aging face and sat in a chair by the wall. I could hear the French women singing faintly, but then I heard another sound coming from behind the wall. It sounded like a chant, and then it stopped. Did my ears deceive me?

"Do not doubt."

The voice from my dream before rang in my ears. I stood up and watched my eyes in the mirror. Now I was remembering what this madness was like. Was it worth it?

I turned to the wall where I'd heard the sound and examined it. I found one geometrical image not matching the others and pressed it. Part of the wall slid to the side, and another hallway was revealed to me. I took out my old, trusted revolver, which I refused to change for a new weapon, and moved forward.

I made a few turns, and then the walls seemed to move, almost becoming a blur. In confusion, I tried to steady myself with a hand on the wall next to me but felt wobbly on my feet. I closed my eyes and sat down. When I opened them, everything was back to normal. Visions?

I cautiously and quietly went around another corner and saw a staircase leading down. From there, I could hear chants. They seemed familiar. Perhaps I had heard them in my dreams?

I descended the steps and stealthily peeked around a corner into an open door. To my surprise, there were three men in the room. Tom Pritt sat in a chair. He was observing a young man who also sat in a chair across from him. The young man's eyes were blank, and he was staring into space. Above him stood a tall man with a hood and sharp, ugly features. He was whispering some sort of lines in an ancient language. The chants were coming from a device.

What were they doing to this man? Brainwashing him? Could the lines the other man was repeating be some from the book I had been told to find?

"Aggtthog fattala!" yelled Tom suddenly. "Dark Dreamer fattala!"

"Ag huggoth, ag fagttheg, nothoggib," whispered the other one.

The young man's body shook violently. Blood started coming out of his eyes, and he fell to the floor, dead.

"Damn it...how the hell did that happen again? Why can't you do it like Mije, Jol?" said Tom angrily to the other man.

"Mije reads straight from the book. He has a connection to the Dark Dreamer."

"Uh...you clean up. I'm going back up."

When he said that, I quietly hurried back upstairs, closed the secret door behind me, and made it back to my table unnoticed, but I could feel the cold sweat on my forehead and my heart beating fast. It was tough catching my breath as well. Well, I wasn't young anymore.

The twins were still enchanting everyone in the room with their perfect smooth voices. I was probably the only person who wasn't feeling relaxed. I was tempted to order a cocktail, but I steadied myself and just got more tea. I focused on calming down my body, stopping my legs from shaking, and bringing my heart rate under control. I tried to concentrate on the music only, but it was too late. I was filled with dreadful thoughts and images. Who was the Dark Dreamer? It didn't seem this was the same thing as Aggtthog.

Once the act was finished, I paid the bill and got up to leave, but Tom again approached me.

"Did you enjoy your visit?"

"Very much, thank you."

He grinned and rubbed his hands together. "Did you find it extraordinary?"

"Hmm, I suppose so."

"Here, many find the experience to be hypnotizing."

He smiled, waved goodbye, and as I left, I wondered if he knew I had found the secret passage.

I got back into the car with Vova and headed home, exhausted.

CHAPTER FOUR

It was hard to focus and concentrate that night. I wondered what steps I could take to find out more if the other place, the Shaman Alley nightclub, did not produce a lead. It was obvious that I also should spy on Tom and watch his movements, but this past day made me realize how physically limited I'd become with age. It was frustrating, but I had to adjust. Trailing Pritt without being detected was going to be somewhat difficult. Nevertheless, I was going to have to do it if my other options didn't pan out.

I sipped on black tea and read some parts of the notes I'd gotten from the young man. There wasn't much else I could add to the equation yet. I'd unearthed a cult that was doing some sort of brainwashing, but for it to work, the words had to be read from this Dark Symphony book, and it seemed to matter who was doing it as well. Evidently, the elusive Mije was the one who had the power.

It took a long time for me to fall asleep, and then I had horrible nightmares again.

"The door will open, the water will split."

The echo-like voice was whispering to me. I saw dark waters opening up. I saw its eyes. They were fantastical, impossible to explain. In them, I could see the darkness of the cosmos, but I could not understand it. The longer I looked, the more horrified I became.

"It is he...."

I recognized the voice of Aggtthog.

"The Dark Dreamer, the Dreamer of Deep Symphony, the bearer of Dark Symphony."

I saw myself in a cage filling up with black water, but I had nowhere to go, no way to get out. I screamed wildly while Aggtthog watched me struggle. In horror, I began to submerge, and all I could see was darkness. All I could feel was darkness.

I sat up in bed, shaking in a cold sweat.

Thankfully Ida did not wake up. It was four in the morning, and I got up and went to sit at the kitchen table and drink some tea. No way I could go back to sleep. Did I even want to?

Shaman Alley nightclub was my next step.

CHAPTER FIVE

The gloomy skies hung above me like a hammer that would never strike but just stayed there, menacing, always a threat weighing on the mind.

I stood in front of Shaman Alley. It was supposed to open only at night, but I had no desire to come to this place after dark. Since I could see someone standing inside behind the glass door, I had hope. I knocked and peered through the glass.

The figure of a man moved towards me, and I could see him clearly. He was tall, with dark skin, long hair, a thin body, long arms, and dark eyes.

He opened the door a bit, annoyed. "We are closed, you see, no?"

"Please, I'm not here for fun. I'm a private

detective. This is about a missing person."

The man's irritated look vanished. "Oh, well, what's your name? I'm Kilop."

He opened the glass door wider, letting me inside and showing me to a chair. He sat down in another one across from me.

There was no point in lying or being cagey, so I got right to the point. "I'm Luc Nistage. I'm investigating the case of a Natalie Larsson. She has gone missing. Do you know her or anything about this?"

"Know? Oh, yes." But that was all he said. He just sat there, staring at me.

I let a few seconds go by. "Well?"

"Well, what? I don't care to keep secrets, but I don't give them for free." Kilop made a dismissive gesture with his hand and then folded his arms across his chest.

Groaning inwardly, I took out some cash and handed it over to Kilop.

Kilop gave a thin, sinister smile. "Look for the town of Lost Anchor, seaside, down south, in North Carolina. It's located on a long island, connected to the mainland by a bridge." He slipped the bills into the inside breast pocket of his jacket.

"Are you saying that's where she is?"

The man shrugged. "I'm saying it's your best bet. You're not the only one looking for missing young people recently. I suggest you stay at the Drift Castle Resort."

I hoped I'd given this repellent man enough money for a few more questions. "Do you know a man named Mije?"

"I did. He hasn't come around in a while. He may be in Lost Anchor. There are no guarantees."

"Do you know of Dark Symphony?"

"I do not touch this subject. Do I know of it? Yes. Do I want to know more about it? No. Those who looked into it all went mad, or they're dead. You will have evil dreams, and not just when you sleep. Your life will be a nightmare. I suggest you drop this case while you're sane, too, Investigator Nistage."

I thanked him for the information and left. I had to tell Ida the bad news: that I'd be going away for a week or so. I hoped she wouldn't worry, but that was a pointless hope. First, as night began to descend, I wanted to stop by the church of St. Therese.

The church was empty, as it often was during non-service hours. Lit candles shone on beautiful icons. I gently sat down on one of the wooden pews and breathed deeply, absorbing the peaceful atmosphere.

What did the town of Lost Anchor hold for me? Surely this was going to be my last adventure, and I had to be certain that I would return to my family safely, but how could I guarantee this? I pulled down the kneeler and prayed. Tears swelled in my eyes. Why was I so driven by this? Why was I ready to rush into a dangerous unknown to help others?

I left the church feeling a bit better, but my conversation with Ida was tough. Fire was in her eyes, but she knew she could not stop me. As always, her love and kindness came through, and she set aside her anger and fear. In the morning, she made me breakfast. We parted that evening.

I had contacted Thompson, and he

absolutely insisted on accompanying me and said his father would send him with funds necessary for the trip. He would not take no for an answer. So together, we boarded a bus heading to North Carolina.

It was a rainy evening. Thompson sat on the seats behind me, reading some magazine. I sat in a double seat alone as well. In front of me sat a stocky older man who was already sound asleep. Across the aisle from me, to my left, sat a tall man with almost fishlike features. He was hideous, with bulging eyes and large, fleshy lips. Tufts of hair splayed out on each side of his head like gills. His features disturbed me, and of course, he turned his head and stared at me.

"How do you do, sir?" he asked in a slow, strange voice. The amphibian-like lips were moving exactly like a fish's would.

I tried to compose my features and be cordial. "Well, doing well. How about yourself?"

"Rainy day, day is good like today...rain, water. Not much sun, so good."

Thompson leaned over the seat to whisper into my ear, "What in the world is wrong with him?"

"And you, young man? Are you doing well?"

"Ye-yes, um, thank you." Thompson slumped back in his seat, obviously feeling abashed.

The strange man went on. "You see things sometimes, in the rain, in the dark clouds, if you pay enough attention. Things only some can see. BUT! Mainly near an ocean, in the dark tall waves."

I groaned inwardly. Why did I have to be involved with this talkative oddball? I supposed it was simply what I attracted at this point; there was no other way around it.

"The ocean provides truth!" he yelled, startling all the passengers. The sleeping man in front of me startled awake with a snort.

After that outburst, Fish Face turned to his window and just sat there silently. I was relieved. I could feel a headache coming on.

The rain became heavier. In the

downpour, the bus had to move slowly and cautiously. This was bound to add hours to the trip.

The fishlike man began making weird moaning sounds, although rather quietly. I was apprehensive. Was he going to have some kind of an attack, or was it just part of his eccentricity?

I looked toward the front of the bus. There was a family of mother, father and two sons, another man about my age, and an older couple. Half of them were asleep.

"Mr. Nistage."

I heard Thompson in the back again.

"What is it?" I asked quietly.

Thompson came close to my ear. "You've seen one of those creatures, haven't you?"

I took a deep breath. "Two, actually. We can't kill them. At least, I don't think so."

"Are they aliens?" I could hear the fear in the young man's voice.

I considered his question. "Well, perhaps. Or maybe they've been around for a very long time. It's possible they were the so-called 'gods' in mythology."

Thompson digested this information. Then, "Be honest with me. Do you think my sister is okay?"

"Thompson, anyone who's been abducted by a cult and been exposed to that book is definitely not okay. But I do believe she is alive, and I do believe we can save her. And others, many others...if we can destroy that book."

"I hope so...." The ugly young man looked dismal as he sank back into his seat, but I wasn't going to sugarcoat anything for him. I needed him to be strong since he had come along. I was no longer a young man. I could not carry myself and another in this case.

I drifted off to sleep myself. As I slowly woke a few hours later, I saw that the rain had become just a drizzle, and we were moving faster.

The road was now close to the wide river. I watched the water, and suddenly an image appeared to me of the face of a horrific creature. Its eyes were closed, and tentacles calmly floated all around me. I shook my head with my eyes closed and looked out again, and there was just the dark water. These moments of madness, surely more of them were going to creep my way as I was going back inside a world of unknown horrors.

In the dark, on slick roads, the bus slowed down again. We were clearly far behind schedule due to the storm, with perhaps four more hours to go.

The fish-faced man across from me was mumbling something again. It hit me then: He wasn't speaking English, but a language similar to the cultist ones I'd heard in the past. I tried to listen, but my aging ears could not pick up much, especially with the sounds of the bus and the rain. I could make out some words, but they meant nothing to me. I leaned back in my seat and stopped trying to decipher it. I was getting tired. The last hours of the trip, I spent drowsing in and out of sleep.

It was a deep dark night when we finally arrived at the station, but at least the rain had stopped. Now Thompson and I had to wait for the local bus, which would take us to Lost Anchor, on an island across a long bridge. I was chagrined to see that the crazy fish guy was waiting for it too. I was not surprised.

"What a blessing," I chuckled to myself.

We sat there in the chilly, light breeze for about half an hour, and then in the distance, we heard the screeching of brakes on an old bus. As it neared us with its weak lights, it rocked from side to side as if its tires were partially deflated. It stopped and the door jammed for a few moments as the pale and thin driver did his best to force it wide.

We finally got inside. There were only two other passengers, and both resembled the fish-faced man who got in after us. As none of them greeted each other, I figured they were not related — or they just disliked each other. Oh well. I could see that Thompson was clearly disturbed already, and I shook my head. I squeezed the cross around my neck. Please, my Father in Heaven, give me strength.

The bus creaked and rocked onto the long bridge. In the distance, across the dark waters, I could see the flashing illumination of a lighthouse. Something inside me stirred. Lighthouses are a symbol of so many things. For me, a beacon of hope but also a light that could attract things of which we wanted no part.

It was hard to see much of the water from my seat on the bus, so I focused on the lighthouse's beacon. Once we got across the bridge and came into town, I was surprised to see a number of people out and about at such a late hour. I figured they were most likely fishermen. I was glad to see they did not look like the fish-faced trio on the bus. An older man with a black beard waved at the bus as he stood by the road with a bucket full of fish.

We stopped, and everyone got off the bus. In the distance, by the cliffs, I could see a building with a large sign saying "Drift Castle Resort." Indeed the building looked like a mini-Victorian castle. Above the bus stop hung another sign, more worn and scratched, which read "Town of Lost Anchor." The word "Welcome" did not appear anywhere.

The young man, Thompson, kept stumping around me, acting lost. I took him by the shoulder and told him to relax, then we picked up our suitcases and began walking down the dark old street towards the hotel, or resort, as they called it.

There was a rugged-looking diner and a bar, which we passed by as both were closed. There were few streetlights and only one light in one small window as we made our way toward the resort. Now we could see the lighthouse on a spit of land in the distance to our left. We then proceeded to our right into the courtyard of the resort.

The building had what looked like dark blue brick walls, several castle-like small domed towers, and small windows. It was located on the cliffs overlooking the ocean. We entered through a thick wooden door and found ourselves in a well-lit lobby.

Behind a long reception desk stood a medium height bald man with eyes that blinked rapidly and rolled around randomly. He spoke very quickly.

"Welcome to Drift Castle Resort. I am Cyan. May I assist you?"

"Yes, we'd like two rooms."

"For how long?"

I took a breath. "Not sure yet."

"Very well. Both ocean view?"

"Not for me," said Thompson.

I looked at him, surprised. I shrugged. "Just one with the ocean view, then."

"Wonderful. You'll love it. Breakfast is included with your rooms. Here you go."

We signed the register, paid for the first night, and he handed us each a key. Both rooms were located on the second floor, just up the flight of wooden stairs.

Thompson looked even more tired than I, an old man. He entered his room quickly and, I assume, collapsed into bed. I searched my room thoroughly first thing. There was nothing suspicious. It was a beautiful Victorian-style room.

I opened the door to the balcony and went out. I not only had an ocean view, but I could see the lighthouse. I stood there for a few minutes watching the dark waves illuminated by the moon, and then I went to bed myself.

Dark dreams invaded my sleep — which was nothing new — but this one was different. I found myself in an asylum, in a long, dimly-lit corridor with locked patient rooms on each side. The doors had small glass windows, and I could see the inmates inside. As I kept on walking, I realized that there was no end in sight, and it all looked similar.

When I looked into one of the rooms, or cells, a man was kneeling facing away from me. He was screaming something frantically.

"Dark Dreamer will awake! His servant is near. He will have the one he needs!"

Then a voice spoke behind me, a familiar one. I turned around, and a tall, dark figure with six tentacles stood in the shadows.

"You are close to me now, but you will lose your mind before you can stop his awakening. My slaves are everywhere. Their eyes will be on you, their ears will listen to you, they will sniff you out, and you will kneel before me."

Then the figure disappeared, the hallway

became pitch black, and I felt water beneath my feet, rising quickly. A moment later, I was drowning, and I felt tentacles around my legs, pulling me down.

I woke up with a scream and sat up in bed. I was sweating, and my old heart was popping out of my chest. Why was I putting myself through this horror at my age? I was a madman, a fool. Ida was right. I belonged at home with my family.

I looked out of the window. The moon powerfully illuminated calm ocean waves. It was enchanting. I watched as long as I could, and then I drifted off again, this time without nightmares.

Chapter Six

Sunrise came without warning, and the rays forced my weary eyes open and shocked them for a second. As I adjusted to the light, I could appreciate the beauty of the ocean and sky and all their changing colors. But I knew the true nature of the water and that it hid terrible things.

I got dressed, and of course, no surprise, I, the old guy, was the first up and had to go and knock on Thompson's door to wake him up. After a few minutes, he opened up, looking groggy.

"Thompson, get dressed and let's have breakfast, then we go check out the town."

He nodded and thankfully got ready in

no time.

We came down the same wooden stairway and were immediately greeted by a thin, tall man. He had short black hair, a narrow face, long skinny arms, small eyes, and a short sharp nose. He wore a slim black suit. It was almost catlike, the way he spoke and moved.

"Hello, gentlemen. I am Ritz, owner of this establishment. Did you have a good first night with us?"

Thompson nodded but remained silent. I was glad that he understood that I was the one who needed to lead conversations.

I smiled. "It was great. Beautiful ocean view. We are excited to explore these parts."

"Father and son adventure?"

"Actually, he is my student, an assistant learning the trade."

"What trade may that be, if you'd don't mind me asking, my dear sir?" Ritz's voice was as smooth as a cat's meow.

"Private investigator."

"Oooh, so this isn't an all-pleasantries type of journey. I do hope you still have time to enjoy all the island has to offer, despite your work."

"Of course, Mr. Ritz. Thank you for the hospitality."

He gracefully gestured toward an open door. "We have a wonderful breakfast right around the corner. Our waiter Kit, who has returned from visiting family, is the best server I've had. I'm glad he's back. You may take a seat and eat as much as you like. We shall speak more another time; let me know if you have any questions."

"Thank you."

I nodded and went into the dining room. We sat down at a table right next to the large window overlooking the cliffs and the calm ocean.

A few gulls appeared in the sky and then slowly and masterfully glided in the wind and circled above the water before diving in to grab unsuspecting fish.

Thompson's mouth opened wide. "Wow, I've never seen that!"

I chuckled. "Nature at its best, Thompson.

Learn from it."

I heard someone approach from behind and turned my head. To my surprise, it was the fish-faced man from the bus. Apparently, he was the brilliant server named Kit, as his name tag confirmed.

"Hello again, and welcome to Drift Castle Resort, sir. What may I get for you?" He held a pen poised above a menu pad.

"Well, I'll have two coffees with milk, pancakes, and two eggs scrambled. Your turn, Thompson."

"Um, a ham omelet, please."

Kit nodded and walked away. Thompson watched him in fascination. Then he turned to me.

"So, how will you investigate? Whom will you talk to?"

"I'll talk to anyone and everyone. We will look for clues, some sort of tells, or nervousness. Suspicious activity. I'll also do a lot of investigation without you—I hope you understand."

"Of course, I'll do whatever you say."

"Great, I'm glad."

Kit brought our food, placed the plates, and stared at me with his strange fish-like eyes. He just stood there. An image of a fish gazing through the glass of an aquarium came to my mind.

Clearing my throat, I said, "Um, thank you, Kit."

He stared some more, then slowly turned and left.

Thompson shook his head. "What a weirdo."

"Wonderful. Most pleasant server ever. As he was the best traveling companion ever." I chuckled.

Thompson laughed at my remark like a kid. Actually, he was still basically a kid. Had I been right to let him come along?

I looked out at the ocean again and started to sip my coffee. I knew this relaxing morning could not be taken for granted. This was possibly about to become another deadly adventure.

I began eating the food. It was simple

but hearty and perfectly prepared. A bird landed right outside the window and stared at my plate, moving its head from side to side. I smiled, and to my surprise, the bird waited until I finished my meal to fly off, disappointed.

On the way out, we saw Kit again. I thanked him for the meal, and he just nodded. Outside the door, the air was cool and fresh, there was a perfect ocean breeze, and the sun was warm on my skin. The older I got, the more I appreciated life's simplest pleasures.

The town of Lost Anchor was very small, and we headed straight for the town hall. On our way there, we passed by a large house made of grey brick with a statue of a mermaid in the front. I wondered to whom it belonged to. Next door was a small shop selling medicine and herbs, then a bar, and then a tiny market with fresh fish on ice out front and the town hall right behind it. It fronted a small square paved with old stones, with a non-functioning circular fountain in the center. Next to it was another statue, this one of a fisherman with a large beard.

"Ye visitors."

We turned around, and behind us was a ragged man with a large black beard, small black eyes, and a very wrinkled, dirty face.

"Ye not from round here."

"No, we are visiting. You are correct."

"Who are ye visitin'? Ya ma? Hahaha."

I tried my best to pretend the joke was funny, but it was tough. I managed one guffaw. Thompson just stared at the man.

"We are here on official business."

"Ooooo, fancy, fancy...oooofficial. Hmm, ye better not be messin' round too much! Or we won't catch enough fish!"

"Why?"

"He don't let us catch fish if ee's angry." The beard swung from side to side as the man shook his shaggy head.

"Who?"

"Ye ask too much. Ye just don't be messing round." He spat on the side of the road and walked away from us. "Ye bastards!" he yelled as he tottered away. I shook my head.

"We call him Old Smith."

The speaker stood on the steps of the town hall. He was tall, with grey hair and a long grey mustache. "I'm Mayor Milton. Don't mind Old Smith. Of course, you are welcome. You have questions?"

"Yes, actually."

"Well, come in. I have an office on the right side of the building." He led us in.

Inside the building was as aged as the outside, no surprise, with old grey columns and a grey floor with some cracked stone squares. We followed Milton to the right corridor and entered a rather small room behind a glass door. He sat down behind his messy desk and invited us to sit in the two chairs across from him.

He smiled at us. "So, what brings you to our lovely and peaceful town? What are your names?"

"My name is Luc Nistage, and this is Thompson Larsson," I said, indicating Thompson, who gulped and nodded. "I am a private investigator, and he is my assistant. We are looking for a young woman. I got a lead indicating she may be in these parts."

Mayor Milton leaned back with a surprised look on his face. I could instantly tell he was play acting. Therefore I was immediately suspicious.

"What is her name? Do you have photos?"

"Natalie." I placed her photo on the table.

"Tsk tsk. That's very sad. So many go missing these days," he said, shaking his head. "Well," Milton went on breezily, slapping his hands on his desk, "I will make sure to let the sheriff know and have him contact you unless you find him first. You are free to look everywhere, of course. I have not seen her, obviously. His name is Jott, Sheriff Jott."

I stood up, knowing we were dismissed, "Thank you for your time." Thompson looked disappointed as we left, but I assured him that in this type of case, such stonewalling was no surprise.

We walked along the town streets. The people of the town looked to be hardworking, simple folk. Some had a very tired and weary look on their faces, especially the men. I could recognize those who had been in the war.

Then I noticed a wooden sign with blue letters announcing the Sea Horse Bar.

"Thompson, from here, you go back to the resort."

He nodded, looking a bit disappointed, but he headed back. I wanted to continue looking for information by myself, and such a bar was perhaps not the best place to let that young man into.

I opened the old wooden door and entered. It took a few moments for my eyes to get used to the dim lights. Few of the tables were taken. To my surprise, no one looked at me except for the man behind the bar. Middle-aged and bald, he had beefy, tattooed arms.

I sat at the bar and ordered black tea. The man gave me a funny scowl and went to get it for me.

"There you go, buddy." He slammed my teacup down in front of me.

I let the unnecessary force slide. "Thank you," I said, smiling pleasantly. "Are you the owner?"

"That's right. Newport is the name. You?"

"Luc, nice to meet you. How long have you had this bar?"

"Since I came back from Vietnam. Five years ago."

Wow, I thought to myself, *it looks like it's a hundred years old.*

Evidently, Newport had seen the expression on my face before. "Oh, that look. Listen, this place was an even bigger dump when I took over, another very old, abandoned bar. I've been slowly improving it. I don't make that much money, you gather?"

"Of course. At least the people here have a public house."

"Oh, these people...they have plenty already, all right."

I tried to keep my tone nonchalant. "You sound like you're not pleased with the town."

"I grew up here. Got married here. After I came back from the war, the place just was no longer the same. It's never going to be."

I was puzzled and intrigued by his

comment. "Why is that? How come?"

"It used to be a town of fishermen, crabbers, shrimpers. For a long time, these traditions remained strong. In the 1920s, they built an asylum not far from here." He shook his head and paced back and forth.

This didn't seem like something that would ruin a town, especially since it had happened forty years ago. "What about the asylum?"

"Well, obviously, it brought a bad reputation here. There were also other strange things and rumors of wrongdoing in that place. My father would often say that it ruined the feel of our place. The asylum was shut down eventually, and Father, in his final years, said that a good atmosphere was here again, but once I came back from the war, I felt that feeling my father talked about again. People began to act strange."

I set down my cup. "How far from here is it?"

"I don't recommend going there for a tour, but if you just go to the west part of our town, you'll see an old sign with a passage leading into the hills among the cliffs. It'll read 'Gregor Mijec Asylum.'"

Chills ran down my spine as I heard the name. My face must have registered something because Newport looked alarmed.

"Are you okay? You look like I said something shocking."

"Oh, no, no," I said, in what I hoped was a neutral tone. "I'm okay. Gregor Mijec? He was a doctor?" *Could "Mije" and Gregor Mijec be the same person?*

"Oh yeah, the head doctor, in charge of the whole place. They say he disappeared, and no one saw him again. But, I dunno, sometimes I feel like there are people in this town who know otherwise." He shrugged. "Or maybe they don't really know anything anymore. I'm not sure."

"Well, Newport, thank you for this conversation. I'll be back."

"I hope you're drinking something other than tea next time," he grinned. "Or now you're too old, eh?" He chuckled at his own little joke.

I smiled, but answered, "I haven't been drinking much for a long time, or at least I try not to. Take care, Newport."

I walked back out into the street. I noticed a few children playing outside an old red brick townhome. On a bench sat a man who was probably still young, but his face was careworn and exhausted, his arms hung down, he had a messy beard, and his eyes were filled with nostalgia as he watched the kids play. At least it was good to see that this town had kids living in it.

I walked by an old store. Its sign said, Boom Market. I looked through the window, and it seemed like a regular simple shop with basic items such as eggs, milk, bread, produce, and meat. On the side of the street was a man calling out, "Fresh fish!" He stood behind a stand with a wooden crate filled with ice and several whole fish. I hoped they were freshly caught today.

So far, I did not need anything and decided to go by the water on my way back to the resort. As the sun began to get lower in the sky and I watched the waves get higher, I thought I saw something out in the ocean. I stopped, almost paralyzed with a sudden wave of terror. Sweat formed on my forehead, and my aging heart began to pound mercilessly against my breastbone. I held my hand above my eyes and peered at the sea. It was someone's, or something's, head. It appeared quickly but then vanished just as fast. I saw it bob up and down several times, and chills ran through my body as I felt its gaze upon me. I could not figure out what this was, and the unknown factor added to the fear. I began to move again. However, I found myself going slowly, and it was harder to move my legs. I turned toward the resort and tried to focus on getting there faster. I could see in my peripheral vision the periodical flash of the lighthouse upon the water, which was darkening along with the sky. Just a little farther!

Finally, I was in the yard of the resort. Breathing heavily, I sat in the nearest chair I could find and began to calm my body down.

"Are you fine, dear sir?"

I heard someone speaking incredibly fast. It was Cyan, the bold reception desk worker.

"Yes, thank you. Just perhaps a glass of water?"

Another man walked out into the yard, short, stocky with black hair.

"Cyan, please hurry with room number 20. I'll assist the gentleman. Hello, my name is Marco. I help Mr. Ritz manage things here. A glass of water or a juice?"

"Sure, a juice."

"Very well, one moment." He inclined his head stiffly and left.

He came back with a glass of apple juice. It was cold and refreshing.

"May I ask what happened, sir?" Marco bent over me in a solicitous way.

I smiled and drank more juice. "Perhaps I forget my age sometimes, huh."

Was it my imagination, or did he look relieved? "Oh yes. Well, let us know if you have any concerns."

Marco nodded to me and left. Hmmm, room number 20. It was an odd time for someone to be checking out of a hotel. Perhaps someone was checking in, and the room wasn't ready? My curiosity was piqued.

When I entered the hotel, I saw only one other person in the lobby. A young blonde woman was sitting by the window and reading. I slowly made my way up the stairs.

At the opposite end of the hall from my room, out of my view and around a corner, I could hear some sort of commotion. I slowly walked over to the corner. Suddenly Ritz appeared, nearly running into me.

"Mr. Nistage, are you feeling well? Marco told me you were a bit tired. You know, your room is actually the opposite way--would you like me to help you?"

Well, if he was going to assume I was a doddering old fool, so much the better. "Oh, my goodness, my head is all in the clouds," I answered. "Of course, it's that way."

"Yes, with the ocean view." He gently turned me in the direction of my room.

"I think I need to lie down and rest as soon as possible."

"Let us know if you need help."

I pretended to be a little unsteady on my feet, then I entered my room, locked the door, and kept the lights off. I sat by my window and stared down at the back door of the resort, hoping to see something. I was following a gut feeling.

I was indeed correct. Eventually, as the moon rose and shone upon the back yard, the ocean and the large rocks at the cliffs, the door opened. I saw Kit emerge carrying a large black bag upon his shoulders. It looked like a body was inside of it. Ritz and Cyan followed. They went to the right side of the resort, turned the corner, and were out of my sight. Were they involved with the cult? Perhaps they were going to meet Gregor Mijec. I dared not follow, but I had an idea of what to do.

I would give Thompson some mundane tasks around the resort and town while I did some real investigating. I decided that the next day I would go to the abandoned asylum and, later at night, hide in the foliage near the resort and watch.

CHAPTER SEVEN

Sleep did not come easily, and when I did fall asleep, I was again entangled in a terrible mental torment of horror.

I tossed and turned, waking frequently. The images were strange, and I did not understand where I was in my dreams. Things spun around me, and constantly a face, which brought feelings of doom, hung before me in thin air. The eyes were closed—he wasn't human, but he did appear to be humanoid. And it wasn't the same being as Aggtthog. I understood, deep inside my consciousness, that this was the Dark Dreamer, a humanoid octopus-like creature, powerful, with an immense aura. Then I would hear the other one's whispers.

"Your journey will end here on these

cliffs, Luc. You will finally meet your end and see the Dark Dreamer awaken. You cannot save the girl. She is chosen for the ritual. The symphony will be read and heard, and you will bleed from your ignorant ears. You will know the enlightenment of the deep. The earthly paradise will welcome you and dissolve your bones in the dark waters."

I finally sat up in bed. It was five in the morning, and there was no way I was going to sleep more. I grasped the cross around my neck, knelt beside the bed, and prayed for my Father in heaven to give me strength to endure the horror one last time. My hands and head became warm. I felt a presence and was encouraged. Tears rolled down my cheeks.

After a long and emotional prayer, I sat by the window and watched the beautiful sunrise for a prolonged amount of time.

"Breakfast, give Thompson tasks, asylum, and then stake out the resort," I said to myself once I felt ready for the day.

After a shower and a shave, I woke Thompson and hurried him, although I was still feeling very slow. On the way down the stairs, I gave him some basic tips, telling him he had to talk to people at the resort and in town, and write down anything he found that sounded important or suspicious.

Kit brought our food and coffee with a surprisingly large, hideous smile. Not pleasant. I wondered if he knew I was suspicious of them.

The first sip of coffee that morning was heavenly and gave me a strong shot of energy. I ate the eggs slowly and made sure I chewed well, but Thompson gobbled up his sandwich almost instantly and then frantically began to shift his eyes from outside to everyone in the eating area. He was already overdoing his simple task. I shook my head.

I got my trusted revolver and parted ways with Thompson. Now it was time to find the asylum. The Gregor Mijec Asylum.

The skies were blue, and the ocean was welcoming. Golden sunshine perfectly laid a coat of heavenly color upon the smooth waves, but I knew what was below.

On my way out of town, I met a few fishermen, young and old. They carried buckets filled with fish.

"Good day ye! Praise the one of the ocean for blessing upon us!" one of the elders said to me. I nodded. The youngsters looked at me with suspicion.

I continued following the passage by the cliffs and saw a boat with a young couple in it. The young lady stretched out in the sun. Her feet were in the young man's lap, and he was rubbing them and smiling. I did not want to look too long and make anyone uncomfortable, so I soon made my way around the bend. There, a tall hill with a white building right on the edge of the coast revealed itself. There was an old sign with some missing letters.

"G eg r Mi e syl m"

This was the place. I looked around, then walked the perimeter. I saw no one. I also noticed some bushes growing by the asylum and a thick, large tree. This was important to note in case I needed to hide. The way the building was placed put me at a disadvantage if anyone came along, and there was only one path out. The other way was the cliffs and ocean. Well, this was what I had come here for. It was no time to let fear set in.

I walked up towards the old asylum. The heavy white door was shut. I pushed on it, and eventually, it slowly cracked open. With more effort, I made enough of an opening to go by. Getting old was no fun at all.

The air was dusty. In front of me stood a worn and broken front desk. The lobby had a few chairs and cracked floors. The once-white color of the walls now was more yellow. Something caught my eye. A large rat sat in one of the corners, and it did not look startled by me. It was used to humans, only when I approached it did waddle into a hole slowly. Was that correct? Was the rat used to seeing people coming in? I began to walk up the flight of stairs to investigate the top floors.

As I got to the next floor and faced a long hallway in front of me, chills ran down my spine as I deeply swallowed and exhaled. It was the same hallway from my nightmares.

It was dark, but enough light was coming from holes in the ceiling and old windows in the back. I still needed to turn on the flashlight to look into each room. As I passed them, my heart was racing. I almost expected to see someone in one of them, but as I went through the entire hallway, all the rooms were empty.

The office had a few old leather chairs, a work desk, and a broken lamp. Then I noticed a circular red rug that looked suspiciously newer than the other things. I swiftly moved it, and underneath it was a door painted with a red triangle filled with strange images. I pulled up on a ring in the middle of it, and it opened without a sound.

I hesitantly shone my light down into the hole and saw a black floor. It didn't seem far to drop, so I shook my head in disbelief that I would do this and jumped in.

I was in a hallway with black walls and floor. I shone my light ahead and saw a red door at the end of the hall. I stood still for a few moments, listening for any sounds. There was nothing.

I approached the door, and it opened with ease. Inside was a room illuminated by several strange blue-glowing jars. In the center of the floor was a larger red triangle. There were unlit candles everywhere. On the walls were shelves, and on them were glass jars filled with what looked like human organs and body parts. They were indeed conducting rituals here. It was time for me to leave.

I managed to climb out the same way I got in, close the door, and cover it with the carpet again. That's when things got eerie for me. I heard the sound of someone walking up the steps at the other end of the hallway, and then I heard voices. I quickly got out of the room and darted into one of the empty patient rooms, where I slid under an old bed. The steps got closer and closer. In the hallway, I could see two pairs of feet. They both stopped. I heard a sinister quiet, and a calm voice like I had never heard before.

"The door...."

"What about the door, oh Great Reader?"

The Great Reader must be Mije/Mijec!

My heart began to pound. I felt myself being sucked into a place of horror, as this man's aura was powerful. I could feel his darkness.

"The door is not at the same angle as I left it."

"It could be the rat? The wind?"

Mijec, who wore black shoes, walked towards the office. I could no longer see his feet.

"Maybe you're right, but my gut feeling rarely lets me down. Let's prepare the room quickly, then we can do the reading by the cliffs first."

As I listened to the secret door open and then shut, I got up and, as quietly as I could, walked across the hallway. With every step, fear was weighing upon my shoulders. What if they saw me now? God, please protect me!

I successfully got downstairs, but as I walked out of the building, I saw several men in black hoods standing down the hill. I dived into the bushes. They weren't looking in my direction, so I was unnoticed, but now I had to stay put for who knew how long.

Eventually, the men got closer to the building. Then three more men arrived, leading a young man dressed in white. He looked rather excited and happy. They placed a chair by the cliffs facing the ocean. He sat in it as they tied his hands and legs to the chair. The young lad quietly watched the waves with a huge smile on his face. Brainwashed and hypnotized, undoubtedly by Mijec.

I was starting to feel spent from all of the mental and psychological pressure. Two hours must have passed. My knees were in pain, and my feet felt numb, but I did not dare to move. Then finally, the door creaked open, and I saw Mijec.

He was a tall bald man with narrow shoulders. His face was thin and void of any emotions. With black eyes, he gazed upon the poor smiling fellow. He then stood in front of the chair, faced the cliffs, and opened a black book. This, indeed, was the coveted and horrific Dark Symphony. All of the hooded followers fell to their knees. He began to read in his low, calm, sinister voice.

"Ashgos, mortios, nee
Nee, taalos
Nee, gathhggo
Aggtthog, igate
Aggtthog, igate!
Ninothgyus
Notroguhts
Hottgguss
Ashgos, mortios, nee.
Aggtthog, igate!
Imggathele, dothggot nee, igate...."

He shut the book rapidly. Dark clouds gathered around the cliffs. The waves became large and violent, and then, as I watched in horror and astonishment, the creature from my nightmares appeared. Aggtthog, The Oracle.

First, his black head emerged. It was covered with scaly skin, but the features were similar to a human's. Then came the long and terrible body. Six giant tentacles and two arms with six needle-like fingers on each hand. He towered over all of them. He spoke, but I could not grasp the sound, or perhaps I was simply too paralyzed with fear. The young man in the chair was still smiling. Then Aggtthog turned his head slightly in my direction. His eyes met mine within the bushes. The horror almost made my heart stop as my body shivered.

Nevertheless, he did not notify the others of my hiding place; he simply smiled. Then with one of his tentacles, he grabbed the young man and slipped him into the water with him. The sky cleared, and the waves calmed. Mijec still stood there watching the waters. One of his followers approached him.

"Was it the right sacrifice?"

"Yes, but there is a more important one. When the blood moon appears, we will bring the girl, and we will awake the One who will usher in a new age. This was indeed a good start. We will perform the ritual the same way, but by the lighthouse, when the blood moon is upon us." Then Mijec stood watching the waves.

The hooded man nodded and moved away. Shortly after, Mijec left and led them all away from the cliffs.

Relief flooded me, but it took me a while to move my legs again, and when I was sure they were trustworthy, I came out of the bushes. My strength was drained completely. I wondered if I still had the strength to spy on Ritz as well, but most importantly, I knew what the goal was now. The girl Mijec had spoken of had to be Thompson's sister. I had to get her away before this so-called blood moon. I had to ask the locals what that could mean and when it was happening. I had to find her before that day came.

As I stumbled back into the town, weary and full of anxiety, I heard a familiar pleasant sound as I walked by a restaurant called Café Chalie. I could hear the sound of a slow jazz song. Beautiful. I noticed a poster featuring a lady and a microphone. It said, "Don't miss Pammi, our special guest jazz singer."

I walked inside despite knowing I should have been heading back to the resort. The place was dark, and only the stage was lit. Only half the tables were taken. I sat at an empty one and ordered wine, even though I knew I shouldn't be drinking.

There she was, Pammi, wearing a blue dress, singing in a smooth and silky voice. The light created a half shadow on her face, which very much resembled a marble statue with blue eyes. Her short dark hair went well along with the minimalist look and stage.

"The waters are blue,
Your darling is waiting for you,
Her heart is in pieces.
She is worried sick,
but there you are in the rain.
Slowly fading, you must not be weak.

The ocean is calling,
For you to wake up,
That courage inside you,
It must be brought out.

The sea waves are strong,
They call out your name,
You are her hero,

So have no delay...."

The words began to fade as my mind began to fade as well. The wine really did me in. I was no longer used to alcohol. I'd had enough. I focused the best I could, paid my bill, and with shaky legs, exited the restaurant.

It was getting dark. I was having trouble balancing. I stumbled and nearly fell when someone grabbed me. It was Thompson.

"Hmmm." He looked at me with grave eyes.

"Thank you, Thompson. I have some big news, but first, I must rest in my room."

CHAPTER EIGHT

I'm sure Thompson was very angry with me for drinking, but he also did not know what I had gone through earlier. In the lobby of the hotel, we ran into Ritz. He said something, but I don't remember what. Then Thompson helped me into my room, and I collapsed on the bed. As I drifted off, I could see him closing the door.

That night I do not remember having nightmares, but when I woke up in the morning, the headache I had was the nightmare. My body felt heavy as I sat up. *I'm too old for all of this*, I thought. There was a glass bottle of water on the side table, and I downed all of it. That made me feel a bit better. I walked to the sink and splashed water on my face. Then I heard a commotion downstairs; someone was yelling loudly. I opened the door. Thompson already stood in the hallway.

"What's going on, Mr. Nistage?"

"Well, let's listen." I walked over to the stairs and leaned over. In the lobby downstairs was a man yelling his lungs out at Ritz and Cyan.

"Where is he? Where is he? I know you, bastards? You sick bastards! I'll bring a whole department from out of town down on you!"

Ritz was making calming motions. "Please, sir, I have no idea where your brother is, I swear!"

The man screamed more and then ran out. Ritz turned and looked up. Our eyes met, and then he gave me a long thin smile. I swallowed as I felt chills run up my arms. He waved nonchalantly and walked off, looking very calm.

We proceeded down, looked around, and saw a few guests looking uncomfortable. Then we sat down in the breakfast room, next to the window, as usual. It was a very clear day. After we ordered from the weird but ever-pleasant

Kit, Thompson told me all he had found out. He had learned a lot of details about the town, and I must say I was impressed. He told me about meeting the sheriff, Jott, and his dumb deputy, Poli. It was an amusing story. Then when he finished, I spoke. His face changed from excited to intense and grim as I mentioned his sister, Natalie.

"Thompson, Mijec is here, and he has your sister. She will be a part of a ritual to wake a being more powerful than Aggtthog unless we can find her before that. We must find out when the so-called blood moon will happen."

I was interrupted by another commotion. I saw Cyan run into the hotel and then hastily run down a hallway. I motioned to Thompson to stay put, and I followed Cyan as nonchalantly as I could. I entered the hallway and saw shadows at the end. I crept close enough to hear Cyan's voice. He was speaking to Ritz.

"Another murder! Another one of ours dead!"

"Calm down! Was it the same method as the first?"

"Yes, throat cut and stabbed in the heart, one ear missing."

"It could be a coincidence. Both wandered alone at night. I doubt he targets us specifically," Ritz said, trying to calm Cyan.

"A serial killer? Here?" Cyan's loud whisper sounded hysterical.

"Well, we are here, aren't we? So why not someone else?"

"I have an idea. Come on."

They walked out of earshot, and I went back to the breakfast table. What had that been all about? I sat back with Thompson and looked at him with some concern.

"We must ask around during the day about the blood moon, but you stay in during the night, got it?"

"You were the one needing help at night, Investigator."

"I promise I will not drink again. Listen, stay in during the night. Understand?"

"Yes. I want my sister back...sir."

"I know. We will do everything we can."

CHAPTER NINE

That day we split up and went around town asking questions. The first place I went was the Seahorse Bar. I ordered a cup of tea to placate Newport and struck up a conversation with him. He seemed irritated today.

"Something bothering you, Newport? Feeling all right?" I sipped the tea.

Newport shook his bald head. "I had crazy nightmares...all night! All night! I woke up in a cold sweat and angry." He shook his head again and wiped the bar aggressively. "This doesn't happen to me often. It's making me exhausted."

Well, that sounded familiar. "What are the nightmares about?" I asked.

Neport frowned. "The moon over the ocean turns red, starts bleeding. There is terrible screaming in my ears. People are dropping dead everywhere. There's blood everywhere. A creature rises from the ocean. The horror of seeing it hurts my heart and shakes my body." He shook his head again, furiously mopping the bar. "How can a dream do that? Even thinking about it makes me feel angry. I don't understand it."

I pondered a moment. "I truly hope it'll pass soon. Insomnia and nightmares can be a very rough experience."

"Damn ye....ah, not you. I mean, just damn it...ah...I'm sorry."

I nearly laughed at his abashed look—it didn't appear to be something he felt often. I assured him there was no need to apologize. Though it was pretty obvious to me that he knew nothing, the description of his nightmare was indeed troubling.

The second place I went was Mayor Milton's office, where, luckily, I did find him. He invited me to sit.

"How may I help you, our dear guest?"

I decided to get right to the point. "Mayor,

what do you know about blood moon rituals? I heard there might be one happening in this area."

A phony smile stretched across his lips, and his eyes gleamed. Milton no doubt knew something.

"Oh my," he chortled, "this sounds more like an astronomy question. Hmmm, never heard of any Lost Anchor residents participating in such a thing."

I wasn't going to get anywhere with him. "Thank you, Mayor." Disappointed, I left. It was pointless to try and squeeze that devious man.

On my way through the street, I saw the crazy old man again. Old Smith. When he saw me, his eyes lit up, and he shook his fist at me.

"Damn bastards! Comin' here, ruinin' simple folk!"

I politely smiled at him and decided to give it a shot. "Say, Mister Smith, what do you know about blood moon rituals?"

He stood there frozen for a minute and then began to scream.

"Thus will come from th' waters! It's swallowin' whole sinners! Death, death and blood to th' bastards! Them cut th' whore's throat, th' blood spillith into blessed waters! He waketh and — "

Then he suddenly stopped, turned around, and ran as fast as he could away from me. Well. That was enlightening.

The third place I went was the Yellow Wave café. The owner was a nice lady named Lakey. I got a pastry and my second coffee of the day and sat down to talk to her.

"Lakey, do you know any traditions around this town that are specific only to here? I heard something peculiar the other day." The apple pastry was flaky and delicious and not too sweet.

She folded her arms across her chest and asked, "Well, young man, what did you hear?"

I laughed at her "young man" remark and took a sip of coffee. "I heard something about a blood moon?"

"Oh, isn't that just when the moon gets reddish in color and gets real big? It looks very nice, but I don't think there is a celebration for it. Maybe some astronomer does a dance?" She chuckled

I smiled and laughed a little too. "Hah."

Then I heard a male voice come from a corner of the café.

"Hey, I might know something."

I turned around and saw a middle-aged man with tan skin, slick black hair, and a mustache. He motioned for me to join him. I picked up my plate and mug and proceeded to do just that.

The man stuck out his hand. "My name is Alphonso. I'm a private eye, just like you." At my raised eyebrows and questioning look, he responded, "Don't be surprised. I could tell by your actions that you're an investigator. I know this region quite well. Although our cases seem different, there must be a reason why our paths have crossed. We can help each other."

I eyed him carefully. "Luc Nistage. Go on, please."

"I know there is a cult in this region. I

also know of a few locations where they meet. My case involves a serial killer, however. I've been tracking him for several years now. His name is Yadek, and there's a very high bounty on him.

"He just committed two murders here. This is the first time he's killed more than one person in the same area. Help me find him, and I'll take you to the locations of the cultists I know. And by the way, the blood moon is in a week, and they always perform major rituals during it."

I didn't have a choice. I had to find Natalie before the blood moon. "All right, I will help you, but you said years, and I have a week."

Alphonso nodded. "You see, I think I know approximately where my guy is hiding out up in the hills. I believe we can track him. I just need to make sure you agree that the bounty is all mine."

I shrugged. I didn't care about a bounty. "That's fine, as long as you take me to the cult's major locations."

The man gave me a penetrating look

and then nodded. "I know where their leader lives. I will show you. Are you ready to track Yadek?"

I put down the coffee mug. "The sooner we go, the better."

"I assume you have a weapon?"

"Yes."

"Great. I was going to head there today myself. I wasn't looking forward to it—the guy's pretty dangerous. It's lucky our paths crossed."

Alphonso insisted on paying for my coffee and pastry, and then we left the café.

Outside, a little way down the street, I saw Old Smith again. He hurried away in the opposite direction when he noticed me.

Alphonso smiled. "That crazy old man. I guess every town should have a lunatic like that. It's some comic relief in hard times."

Considering my own advancing age, I couldn't exactly agree. "I suppose. I'm an old man too. Maybe I'm crazy as well."

Alphonso gave me a puzzled look.

"So tell me, Alphonso, why has this

Yadek been so elusive?" I asked.

The man shrugged. "No one is sure. Some other investigators told me he isn't human. Of course, men will project something extraordinary into the picture when they can't logically explain things. I believe he is just a man, but one with great survival instincts."

"Has he killed other investigators before?"

"Three of them."

Not what I wanted to hear.

Sensing my concern, Alphonso quickly reassured me. "Don't worry, I have a good feeling about this. I, too, have the instincts, and mine tell me that we will get him."

"So what now?"

"We go to my motel, and I'll fill up a backpack for us with food, water, and first aid kits."

"So you are confident you know the place?"

He nodded. "I've scouted the forest path, and I saw signs of someone living up there. I circled and have determined approximately where he is. There are abandoned cabins around there, and I'm sure he is in one of them."

Nothing for it but to follow Alphonso's plan. "Fine, fine, let's head to the motel."

He nodded and motioned with his hand for me to follow him down the street. "You like cigars, Luc?"

"Not particularly, no."

"Not even before such a nerve-wracking experience?"

Oh, brother. I guffawed. "If you only knew what I've been through."

"Huh! I see. So how did you cope?"

"Early in life, with drink. Then with God. And sometimes I didn't cope at all."

"God? Did he answer your prayers?"

"Certainly."

Alphonso was silent for a moment. "That's interesting. You are very confident about that. I'm religious myself, but I have many doubts."

"So do many others. It's hard to live without doubts. That's where faith comes in."

"Hmm, indeed. Well, here we are." He

pointed at a small motel with about six ground-level rooms. "I'm in number 4." We walked up to the door, and he unlocked it with a big brass key. "After you," he said, opening the door.

The air in the tiny room was stuffy. The walls were poorly painted, and the carpet was dirty. Alphonso smiled. "Two years chasing this guy. I had to budget very carefully."

He then took a backpack from behind the bed and started gathering some things from the room. A packet of beef jerky. A glass bottle filled with water. Some bandages and disinfectant. He also had two hunting knives. He handed one to me. His had a beautiful wooden handle with an expertly carved fox, and the one he gave me featured a wolf.

Alphonso smiled down at the one in his hand. "My father's — well, my late father's. He was a good man. He died on a hunt. He was a hunter 'til the end...and what are we if not hunters in a way?"

"Hunters of evil...."

"That's you," Alphonso said, sheathing the knife in a holster attached to his belt. "Me,

I'm not sure. I hunt for the money, yes, but that's not all of it. Maybe it's in my blood."

"Maybe today you'll find out more about yourself," I said, accepting the leather sheath he handed me for the knife.

"You're right. Well, Mister Nistage, ready?"

Ida would certainly disapprove. "Yes, Alphonso, let's get this done. Then I'll need that information."

"Of course, I am a man of my word." He lifted the pack and slung it over his shoulders. "You will know where to go, and in fact, I may help you as well."

I doubted that he'd want to get involved in my investigation, but I felt he was a genuine character. Still, I was going to be careful. He'd handed me one of his knives, but I knew better than to completely trust strangers.

We left the motel and circled around to the back of the building, where the tree line began. Alphonso pointed towards a very tall hill covered with trees. It was almost as intimidating as a mountain. Then he pointed to an opening among the trees close to us.

"The path into the forest starts through there. Then, we will go straight for the cabins up on the hill, but we will have to be quiet and cautious when we get close."

"I think I'm slow either way at my age." I chuckled.

"Haha, you'll do fine. You ain't a grandpa, and you're still a young man at heart."

"Oh, I don't know about that."

He proceeded to lead me into the forest. I scanned the area nervously. I saw no one, but for some reason, I felt eyes on me. Perhaps it was just the adrenaline rush before a dangerous, difficult encounter. I tried to shake it off.

The sky, which had been bright and friendly earlier, began to cloud up, and the forest helped create more gloom. It was lush and rich with variety.

We made our way through as carefully and silently as we could. Every crack of a branch or shaking of a bush alarmed us. A bluebird landed on a thin branch above us and stared in curious observation, then it chirped and flew away. There were plenty of squirrels around, scouting for any food they could find. A line of red fungi was just to my left as we began to go up the hill.

The sky got even darker, and this was concerning. I hoped there would be no rain. I could feel the breeze all the way from the ocean.

Suddenly I thought I saw a flash not too far from us among the trees. We both immediately crouched down and watched for several minutes. Alphonso looked at me, puzzled.

"What the hell was that, Luc? You saw that, right? It was like the air flashed and opened up."

I shook my head. "I didn't really understand what that was, myself. Everything seems calm now."

I was already breathing very heavily. Aging is definitely not something for private investigators. It isn't fun when the mind does not match the body!

Alphonso was moving quietly but swiftly, and I was trying my best to keep up without complaining. This was a life-and-death situation, and there was obviously something strange going on in this forest. Did it have something to do with this killer, Yadek?

I couldn't tell whether the time dragged or went by too fast. I couldn't help but feel certain confusion. I saw Alphonso sit against a tree and take water and meat out of the bag. I sat next to him and had a few sips but refused the meat. Alphonso looked at his pocket watch.

"Three hours now. It sure doesn't feel like it, but it makes sense. I feel tired, but the cabins are not far from here."

I couldn't believe it. "It's been three hours? Wow...I feel a bit confused."

Alphonso took another swig from the water bottle. "That's what they all say when going after Yadek. Just focus on each moment at a time, and we will get him by staying in the moment."

I remembered him telling me earlier that some believed this Yadek wasn't human. I was starting to think that particular theory wasn't so farfetched.

Alphonso got up, and now he was consistently staying in the cover of the trees. I followed him in the same exact fashion, huffing and puffing like that damn loser wolf from the fairy tale. I couldn't get to those cabins soon enough.

As we continued through the oppressive forest, once again, suddenly, there was some sort of a flash, or rather an opening, which appeared just for a split second on my right side. I saw Alphonso dash to the nearest tree. He had a deep cut on his cheek, and I saw a knife that appeared to be made of blue light stuck in another tree's trunk. Sweat ran down my face as I, too, pressed my back against a tree and shivered in horror. I swallowed nervously; my mouth was dry. I had my revolver ready to fire. Perhaps Yadek wasn't human after all...or perhaps he was a human who knew something we didn't.

Alphonso stared at me, looking frantic. "What the hell was that?"

"Focus," I answered.

"What is that?" His composure was

completely gone.

"Focus, Alphonso, focus," I said, firmly. "If you see an opening again, move from the spot you're in."

Another flash and we both dived for cover. Another knife was now stuck in a tree, this time in the spot I had been standing.

"Lead to the cabins, Alphonso!" I whispered, as loudly as I dared. "Go!"

He began to run, and the adrenaline rush from the fear helped me keep up with him, even at my age. Terror could be useful sometimes too. There was another glimpse of light to my left, and I saw a knife fly by Alphonso's head, coming within inches of killing him.

It began to rain, something I dreaded even prior to the situation getting so awful. The black ground became unstable and slippery as we were making our way up. Another light, but this time it was harder to see.

The rain was getting thick, but we finally came upon the first cabin. Alphonso ran in, and I followed, shutting the door behind him.

It was a simple old log cabin. It did look

like it had been occupied recently, for on the table lay some newspapers which did not seem old, and right next to them was half of a red apple. Alphonso sat on the floor and pressed his back against the wall. He had a cut on his arm.

I breathed heavily. "As long as there are two of us, I doubt he will appear inside the cabin, so let's tend to your wound." I opened his backpack and quickly disinfected the cut, and then I tied a white bandage around it. Alphonso shook his head and spoke to me.

"Listen,. Luc, listen..." He took a deep breath. His eyes looked hopeless. "In Dockam town, north of here, there stands a large house. It's where Mijec, the cult leader, lives. Dockam town, you remember that name if you survive this somehow. I'm sorry." He closed his eyes and slumped down.

"I signed up for this knowing the danger, don't be sorry. Try to focus. If you see an opening in the air, shoot. That's our main hope. We will have to move from this cabin soon, and the only way to get out of this is to kill him. We can't stay inside forever. It's just us versus him out here." I set my mouth in a grim line. "We wait 'til the rain lets up, then we go."

"Yes, I agree. That's the only way, but we've got to hope that happens before dark."

"If not, we wait 'til morning. We can't get him in the rain, there just isn't enough visibility, and we can't focus."

Alphonso was clutching his arm. "How about him?"

"I doubt such a thing matters to him. He wounded you while you ran in the rain."

"Yeah." Alphonso looked at the cross around my neck. "The end is not really the end, right?"

I managed a smile. "No, everything will be okay."

"I'll see my family again if it ends here." His eyes were closed.

He seemed to gather himself after saying this, and we both sat quietly, waiting for the rain to stop. Such times can feel like they drag on for an incredible length of time, while in reality, it is not long at all.

I slowly lifted my head above the table and looked at the window covered in raindrops. I focused my old eyes and looked beyond the glass. There, among the trees, I saw the silhouette of a man. He just stood there by one of the trees, all in black. He was human, all right, but I was certain he had some kind of weird special ability. But who knew exactly what that ability was? It seemed to include opening portals between spaces, tearing through from one spot into another in a blink of an eye. Time travel? It was hard to comprehend, and perhaps someone else would not even have believed this, but after everything I had seen and been through, I couldn't dismiss it as impossible.

I blinked, and when I looked again, he was gone. The rain began to lighten up, and eventually, it stopped. There was still a good amount of light outside. My heart began to pound like a drum in the hands of a madman soldier marching into battle. I tried to calm my nerves, but a cold sweat appeared on my forehead. I looked at Alphonso, and his face was once again filled with dread and angst. He knew the time had come. Soon it was going to be us or Yadek, and that was the only way. We crept up to the door. A look of understanding passed between us.

"On three, ready?" he whispered.

CHAPTER TEN

"One...two...three!"

We pushed the door open and ran toward the nearest trees. A moment later, there was once again a flash in the air. Alphonso shot in that direction, but nothing happened. There was a blue light knife in the ground near his feet. We moved among the trees, frantically looking around. The revolver in my hand was shaking as I tried not to stumble while focusing on what was happening around me. Another flash! Alphonso screamed after taking another shot. He collapsed on the ground, and one of the knives was sticking out of his upper chest.

I crawled over to him. His fading eyes were filled with terror.

I gritted my teeth. I recklessly ran towards the next cabin, and as I got closer to it, a knife struck the side of the door. I opened it and got in, quickly shutting the door. Then I hit the floor and crawled toward the back wall, and sat there with my revolver. My heart was pounding so hard that the crazy sound filled my ears. I was staring into space, breathing heavily.

"He will come for me now. He will come soon...." I squeezed the cross around my neck and began to pray silently. One person could only handle so many of such terrors in one lifetime.

A flash! An opening in the air! I shot! A knife hit the wall near me.

Then Yadek stepped out of the air, his body swaying. I had struck him! He produced another knife, but I unloaded the rest of the bullets in my revolver into his chest. His head flipped back, and with a strong thud, his body hit the floor. He lay there, not moving. Dead.

"Mortal like us...after all."

I got up very slowly, as my legs were shaking terribly from the fear and nerves. I couldn't stay there too long; I had to get back before the sun went down. So I left the cabin and began to stumble my way through the trees back to the town.

Going down was much faster, but I was so exhausted it was very difficult. I felt remorse for leaving Alphonso's body behind, but I had to get back before I collapsed.

I was about halfway back when it got dark, and the horrific visions began. It was as though I were having a nightmare, but with my eyes wide open. I began seeing deformed faces in the trees. The ground started moving in spirals. I kept misstepping, and my head began to ache terribly. I felt a strong ocean breeze and whispers from the waters carried into my ears.

"Your time is coming. You and the sea will be one soon...."

Chills ran down my spine and along my arms. It took every bit of my strength and concentration to keep stumbling along towards the town. Inside my head, I began to hear the screams of sirens and the cries of mad, strange birds. In the dark trees, all kinds of eyes began to appear, with triangles inside where the pupils should have been. I grabbed my cross tightly and continued.

"You have never let me down...no matter how hard the journey has been," I prayed aloud, fervently, until I was clear of the forest and into the parking lot of Alphonso's cheap motel. Then I fell to my knees, shaking.

"Ye damn fool!"

I heard the voice of the madman Old Smith. I looked up, and there he stood, but once our eyes met, Old Smith ran away into the dark street.

I got back up onto my feet. "Just a little more to the resort," I chanted to myself and forced my legs to get going.

I walked past the motel and turned into an empty street. There was one light pole, old and damaged but still casting a small pool of light on the sidewalk. Again my vision became a bit blurry. I made it to the pole and held onto it for dear life as I took deep, steady breaths. Then I noticed someone in white standing at the side of the dark street.

"Oh no...it's been a while."

Inside my head, I heard a calm voice as the figure turned and walked away into the darkness. "It's not your time yet. Fight on, live."

I swallowed and felt my heart begin to beat more steadily. "I will be fine. I am fine now. I feel no pain, no fatigue. I am strong," I told myself and started walking again.

I kept repeating this over and over again inside my head as I walked the streets. I felt my step getting quicker, and my focus was regained. I walked by the jazz place and heard lovely music wafting into the street, enticing me, but I did not stop.

Finally, I made it to the resort.

I went straight to my room, ignoring something Cyan was telling me. The moment he heard my step in the hall, a deeply concerned Thompson flew out of his room. I knew I looked worse than I felt because of the shocked look on his face.

"It's all right. I am okay," I quickly assured him. "I do have vital information. But I need to rest first." He nodded. I entered my room, closed the door, and collapsed upon the bed, absolutely spent.

In my dream...yes, a dream! Not a nightmare! In this dream, I saw myself sitting with Ida at our coffee table. She smiled at me and looked content and happy. I sat there drinking coffee, looking back at her with love. I felt as if a huge weight had been lifted off my chest...but then I woke up. The sun was up.

The exhaustion from the night before had really gotten me. I showered quickly, and then I met Thompson — who had been up for some time — in the hallway as usual.

"You might want to see something," Thompson said, gesturing toward a window. "Ritz is talking to someone in the backyard. He's an odd character."

I looked out the window. And to my surprise, the odd character was Tom Pritt, the flamboyant man from the club in the city. He wore a bright red suit, and his hat had a feather. He was clearly unhappy about something.

I told Thompson to stay put and went downstairs. There I crouched down near the back window and cracked it open just a little in hopes of hearing them.

"Ritz, you told me on the phone that Lara is for my establishment!"

Ritz was trying to get Pritt to calm down. "I already told you, it doesn't matter how much you yell, it wants it, so that's a done thing, you know? You don't understand?"

"Don't you feel pathetic obeying some… thing? That's not even an elder being? Just a monster!"

I had to strain to hear what Ritz said next as he dropped his voice, evidently trying to get Pritt to do the same. "With the way you are yelling, we might as well make mimeographs and give one to every guest! Get yourself together, man. It's a done thing, I tell ya. Done thing."

Pritt's voice did drop too, but it was filled with fury. "We will see! I'm staying in town, and I'll talk to her." He turned on his heel and walked away.

"Don't do something extremely foolish, okay?" Ritz called after him.

Tom spat on the ground and never missed a step.

What was Ritz referring to? The ceremony I had seen them perform the other night? Were they giving more humans to some primitive sea monster to devour? That had to be it. I rubbed my head.

In that case, I had to find this Lara. I believed she was the blonde lady I had seen at the resort recently; someone had called her name. At least, I thought so. Did I have time? It was morally right to try, but only this one day.

I had to get back to Thompson and tell him what had happened the day before. I was glad to sit in the breakfast room with him and eat my regular meal and drink a cup of coffee.

Kit looked particularly happy. I wondered what he knew. When the waiter left us alone, I spoke to Thompson.

"Let me tell you what the plan is for today. We don't have much time for anything."

Thompson nodded and leaned forward, looking focused.

"I know now with certainty that Mijec

has your sister. I also know where he lives. I will need to go there.

"There are several scenarios that could play out." I counted on my fingers. "One. I could free your sister if she's there. Two, I could kill Mijec. Three, I could possibly steal the book to leverage it against your sister's life. All possibilities are on the table. There is another pressing issue I need your help with. Ritz plans to kill a young lady tonight, and I want to stop him."

Thompson's eyes were huge. "That's a lot to take in."

I had to smile a little ruefully. "Yes, of course. I'm sorry, young man; this is difficult, I know."

I took a sip of my wonderful hot black coffee. Poor young fellow, I thought. To be relying on an old-timer like me. Why? Not because I'm the best but because I was the only one foolish or daring enough to take on the case.

"Eat, Thompson, eat."

My brain was fully awake after the rough

day before, and I had full control over my skull and body again.

I took a deep breath. "Thompson, pray a lot, okay?"

"I do, Mr. Nistage, I do."

Our eyes met. "I hear the desperation in your voice, the sadness."

Tears filled the young man's eyes. "I would die for my sister. I'd give everything and anything to save her. God only knows how much anxiety I've been hiding."

I had to bolster the kid's faith. "So, trust that God will help save her. Knock, and the door will open."

Thompson nodded, but the look on his face betrayed his doubts. Poor lad, I could really tell that he, indeed, was ready to give his life for his family. I had to admire such strong nobility and honor and so much love. I finished my last few drops of coffee and stood up, feeling my vertebrae cracking into place.

"All right. Thompson, stay around here for now and keep an eye on the employees. I'm going out."

I looked outside as I said that, for the sky had become much darker. Indeed there was a huge black cloud hanging over the ocean in the distance. It made the water look black.

In all honesty, I did not have a specific place in mind. I was trying to stay positive and get my plans clear in my head. As I walked down the town's streets, more or less lost in thought, I saw Tom Pritt on the other side of the street, walking with great haste. He had his head down and looked like he was mumbling angrily to himself. Hardly minding his surroundings, he turned into another street. Obviously, he knew his way around here.

I followed as closely as I dared, doing my best to not be noticed. Tom went up a curving path and then entered the yard of a very nice-looking house. He walked up onto the porch and hammered on the door. I crouched down behind the shrubbery lining the path.

"I'm telling you! You listen to me! Open up!"

After a minute, the door slowly opened, and in the doorway stood Ritz. He had a calm and cool smile on his face.

"Okay, Tom. Come in and have a drink, or even better, since there doesn't seem to be any rain in these beautiful black clouds — a miracle — let's sit in the back yard."

Tom followed Ritz around the house. Once they were out of sight, I sneaked up to the house and edged around it until I could hear them. I carefully peeked around the corner of the house. Tom sat at a wooden table, and Ritz had just disappeared into the back door. Presently he returned with a bottle of whiskey and two glasses. Ritz remained standing close to Tom. He poured each of them a finger of whiskey and began to sip his.

"Ah yes, beautiful black clouds. Tom, how well do you know Mije?"

"Not well enough, I suppose. He gives me the creeps." Pritt took a large gulp of whiskey.

Ritz swirled the whiskey in his glass and chuckled, shaking his head. "Tom, you have a lot to learn. You see, like a spider makes a web, so do the great ones in the waters create their own web of people. People who have their assigned tasks. Mije has a major task, I have my own task, not as big, and you...you have a very small task."

Pritt started out of the chair. "Hey...you promised — "

Ritz put a hand on his shoulder and pushed him back into his seat. "Listen, listen. Do you think Mije is weak? Do you think they are weak?"

"Of course not!"

"There is order and a plan. You understand? Each movement must go in the correct order. Many times they wanted to use the humans, but every time there was some mistake, a flaw in the end, a weak link. You see?"

"Yeah...." Tom swallowed whiskey uneasily and grimaced. His hands were shaking, and his nervousness was showing. Yet again, he was defiant. "Ritz, you said before you didn't need this girl. That I could use her in my businesses. But now she's essential to you?"

There was a beat. "Are you calling me a

liar?" Ritz asked in a smooth, dangerous tone.

Pritt's nervousness became more acute. "No, no, just you changed your mind, yeah? I wish I could have her."

Ritz's expression turned ice cold as his eyes grew lifeless. He casually strolled around Tom's chair and stood directly behind him. Tom kept his eyes on his whiskey glass, but his body was tense.

Then, with a sudden fast and brutal movement, Ritz stabbed Tom in the back of his head. Tom's body went limp and slumped onto the table, with the knife sticking out of the back of his head and blood pooling on the wood.

I stood there with my heart thudding so hard I was afraid Ritz would hear it. Calm down, calm down, I willed myself. I pressed my body against the wall of the house and steadied my breathing.

Ritz, meanwhile, stood there staring at Tom's lifeless form. From time to time, he would raise his glass of whiskey and sip. After a while, Kit appeared.

"Master? What do I do with him?"

"Dump his body in the pit, then feed the girl to our friend."

I was horrified. Still, I quietly rounded the house to watch Kit as he moved a large truck into place. He entered the house and carried out a girl. Lara? She was tied up, with a gag on her mouth and a blindfold over her eyes. He placed her in the passenger seat. Then he wrapped Tom's body in a tarpaulin and put it in the truck bed, among many other things, and threw another tarp over it all. Then he went back into the house.

I knew it was my only chance. Staying low, I quietly ran over to the back of the truck and climbed in, wedging myself in beside some bags of who knew what and covering myself with an old blanket.

The truck's radio played old-time music, loud, as Kit drove. It was not long before he stopped. I held my breath as he yanked back the tarp, but evidently, he didn't notice me under the dirty blanket. I heard him drag Pritt's body off the truck, and I peeked over the side to see what was going on.

I could see a large pit filled with ashes and the charred remains of furniture and bones that could possibly have been human. I shuddered as Kit poured gasoline on the body and tossed it into the pit, and then threw in a lit torch. He laughed as he watched it burn.

Then he got back in the cab, and the truck was moving again. I could only assume that the next destination was the shore.

What was I doing? What was my plan? And why had I gotten myself into this situation at my age? Hiding in the back of a psychotic killer's truck, about to encounter some kind of horrifying creature — and I had to save a young woman from certain death. Would the Lord, my God, protect me? After all, I was trying to save a life. And what about my wife and son if this is the end for me? Would they even know what had happened?

The truck stopped, and I could hear the waves crashing and hissing. Adrenaline coursed through my body, and I threw off the blankets and the tarp and hopped out the back of the truck before Kit, who moved pretty slowly, was even out of the driver's seat. The door was rusty and screeched as Kit opened it, so the sound fortuitously covered any noise I had made. I dived into some brush and had my revolver in my hand as I watched Kit take the bound and gagged girl out of the truck.

The fish-faced man was oblivious to me as he tied the girl to a large rock by the water. Then he pulled from his pocket a circular golden item on a long chain and swung it into the ocean like some kind of lure. He opened his mouth and began to scream insane chats in a strange language. The girl struggled with her bonds but did not make a sound.

What was I doing? I couldn't wait for the creature to show up! I stood up and shot Kit in the back. His body jerked, and he turned toward me with an astonished look on his face. Then I shot him in the head. His body collapsed.

I grabbed the gold chain and pulled the round object out of the ocean. Breathing heavily, I ran to Lara and yanked off her blindfold and gag. Then I took out my pocketknife and began slicing at the thick ropes that bound her to the rock. Behind us, the waters began to bubble.

Horror seized my heart. The creature was coming! Lara looked desperate and confused.

"Please help me. I want to go home...I want to go home!"

"I will. You will go home...just a minute longer, don't panic."

I finally cut through the ropes. I fought rising panic as the noise from the ocean grew louder.

Lara screamed, and I knew she had seen the creature. Then the rope gave way, and I frantically cut off the twine that bound her ankles. I dragged her to her feet.

"Run, girl! Run!"

I had to shove her as I felt the ground shake from heavy steps. I didn't look back. We ran, filled with adrenaline, back to the truck. Kit had left the keys in the ignition, and we got in, and I started the engine. As it roared to life, I stomped on the gas and headed for the road at breakneck speed.

I had to glance in the rearview mirror. On the shore stood a large black scaly creature with four legs and a mouth that was similar to a crocodile's, just larger and longer. The girl was looking out the window at the creature, a look of utter horror on her face. She sat back and stared out the windshield in a state of shock.

"Where are you from?" I asked, hoping that it didn't sound too harsh.

"The...the...city...," she answered in a whisper.

I pulled over and stopped the truck. I took out my pen and tore a sheet out of my notebook, and began writing. The girl looked at me, fearful and confused.

"I am going to buy you a bus ticket and give you some cash so you can eat and get home." I handed her the paper. "When you get to the city, take this paper to the police department and give it to Inspector Listrom. He is a friend of mine. This is information for him about you and Ritz. Okay? Do you understand?"

The fear in her eyes faded a little. "Y-yes. Thank you...I don't even know your name."

"Luc Nistage...I'm glad to be able to

help."

I began to drive again. I took Lara over the long bridge onto the mainland and to the bus station there. It took time, but I felt it was worth it. I bought her the ticket and gave her some cash. I sat with her on a bench for a while, trying to calm her and waiting for the bus. As she began to feel safe, the terror left her eyes. When the bus arrived, she turned to me and embraced me.

"Thank you, thank you, Luc. I will never forget you."

"God bless you on your journey back, Lara."

She got on the bus and waved to me. The bus began to move. For me, it was time to get back to the crazy town across the bridge.

I was driving Kit's death truck and knew I had to leave it a good distance away from the town, so no one would notice me. As I drove, an idea came to my mind. A mad idea, but it took hold of me.

Alphonso, God rest his soul, had told me that Mije lived on the outskirts of the town of

Dockam. Since I already had a car, I made up my mind to go there as the day began to wane. I got across the bridge, and as I turned towards the road away from Lost Anchor and toward Dockam, a deer ran out into the middle of the road. I slammed on the brakes and stopped in time. A beautiful buck with large antlers stared at me with startled eyes, then took off into the woods on the other side of the road.

I had to pay close attention. It was twilight, and there were no lights on this stretch of highway.

Finally, I saw another sign telling me it was one mile to Dockam. My heart was already starting to race in anticipation.

I parked the decrepit death truck among the trees at the northern part of Dockam's outskirts. I wasn't far from the shore, and just in a few minutes, I came out onto a path that ran right along the cliffs. The half moon created enough light for me to see the path without using my flashlight. This was important since the last thing I needed was to draw attention to myself. I could see what I thought was the outline of a large house upon a hill, but I had to be closer to be sure it was Mijec's house.

I stopped for a moment and leaned on a tree. I watched the dark water move calmly. The sky became dark and clear, and a multitude of stars appeared. What a beautiful world. I looked back upon the path and re-loaded my revolver, wondering if these would be my final moments on Earth, my final adventure. I thought about Ida and my son. And I prayed: Please, my Lord, my God, see me through to the end safely, despite my being a foolish man.

I began walking again, focusing on my breath and calming my nerves. I could feel my age. My legs were heavy, and my hands trembled slightly. My shoulders throbbed, and I had a tiny headache coming on. Nevertheless, I breathed deeply and determined that my path was fixed, and there was no turning back.

What was a human life worth anyway? I thought as I trudged. I could have died so many times in my life. Even today. Was it my God keeping me safe? Or is a guardian angel helping me complete these deeds?

I could see the outline of the house very clearly now. It was indeed a mansion. There was no hint of light within it. Was there no one home? My heart lifted a little Perhaps this was for the better. Could I possibly find the book? Well, I was soon to find out.

I stayed in the shadows of the trees as I carefully circled the mansion. There was a path on the right side of the house lined with trees on both sides, leading to a side entrance. I thought it would give me the best coverage, so I slowly made my way toward the house, all my senses on alert. I could not afford any mistakes. Better safe than sorry — an expression that had never had a larger meaning for me than it did now. I was old, slow and tired, and a mistake would cost me my life at this point.

I carefully approached the mansion and looked in the windows. There wasn't much I could see. There was not one light that was on.

Suddenly I felt my heart burn, and I sat down, leaning against the clapboards. I rubbed my chest and tried to calm down further, and when the burning and pain went away, I glanced to my left and saw a cracked-open side door. This was a stroke of luck indeed. At least, I hoped so!

I entered the house carefully and quietly and stood next to a wall, trying to make out the dark shadows of various pieces of furniture. I saw a large globe in the center of the room and a statue of a sea creature, but there were no books.

I decided to turn on my small flashlight and began a closer examination of the house. I took a few steps and stopped as I inched my way along, listening for sounds that I was not alone. All I could hear, though, were the sounds of the wind and the waves. However, I still kept my flashlight shielded and pointed at the floor.

I went from the first room into the next, and there I saw a pile of books on one of the side tables and a whole wall of books on my right. But before I searched here, my gut instinct told me to go upstairs. So I left the room by a door that seemed to lead into the foyer of the house.

I walked up the dark, curving staircase,

shining my light on some of the paintings on the walls. They were all depictions of sea monsters and ocean-dwelling creatures.

Once upstairs, I noticed two narrow red lines drawn on the floor leading to the last door at the end of the hallway. I slowly and timidly followed, praying in my head for no one to come back. Suddenly my vision blurred slightly, and it seemed as though the lines twisted. I leaned up against the wall to steady myself.

"Gah nagym fathagi, suthoggoth."

I heard a voice whispering inside my head. Suddenly an outline of the creature with six tentacles flashed before my eyes. I sank down and forced myself to acknowledge the hallucination. Aggtthog, that was him. I felt a cold sweat on the back of my neck, and my knees trembled. I took many deep breaths, and then everything around me was back to normal. I picked up the flashlight, which I had dropped, and proceeded towards the door. With utmost care, I pushed it open.

The room was almost empty except

for a black altar. It had a statue of a strange tentacled creature. The floor was covered with red symbols. I walked up to the altar and began examining it. I noticed an odd line on the body of the creature. I pressed my fingers into it and tried to pull it apart. Indeed the statue opened up. Inside of it lay a thin black book, the same one I had seen Mije holding. The Dark Symphony, this was it!

With trembling hands, I picked up the cursed book. I felt burning in my fingers. I quickly placed the book inside my coat.

I should have been cautious getting out of there, but my mind was too panicked as I rushed down the stairs and back through the rooms and the door I had entered through. Lucky for me, no one was there. I was still alone when I got outside. There was a strong, cool breeze coming from the water. I didn't waste any time and got away from the mansion and hid myself in the trees near the cliff path. There I caught my breath and calmed my racing heart once again. I had the book!

It took me a long time to make my way

down the path because I stayed inside the tree line, but that was a safer way to proceed. It was a good thing I was staying out of sight because halfway down, I heard a car approaching. I sank deep into the bushes and sat in silence.

As the car got closer, I could hear voices. The bald cult leader, Mije, was driving. "Damned fisherman, I should have been sleeping, resting before all the preparations, yet I had to go down there! And for what?" he yelled.

"He is not a smart man like you, Master."

"Not smart...hah...that's putting it mildly. What was he thinking? Oh...wait. He probably doesn't think. Saw a great fish and reacted."

"Yes, confused."

"Not sure how stupid you have to be to confuse the teachings!" Mije growled, and the car passed by.

I hadn't realized I was holding my breath. I let it out in a sigh and hoped Mije slept downstairs. I had closed up the statue before I left, but he could go and check on it before going to bed, and realizing the book was gone, have his men crawling all over the place.

I got up and hurried on, still sticking to the cover of the shrubs and trees. *Come on, old man, move like you once could!* I said to myself. My heart beat frantically as I ran over the worst-case scenarios in my mind. My Lord, my God, please see me through safely to the end, I prayed fervently.

Amazingly I got back to the truck without further trouble. The surroundings were quiet. I could only hear an occasional night bird and, of course, the waves. Somewhere inside those waves, the dark waters, a great dangerous entity dwelled, asleep, and it had to stay asleep.

I started the truck and drove back towards Lost Anchor and the resort. A plan formed in my mind, but would it work? A simple question. I tried to anticipate everything that could go wrong.

When I reached Lost Anchor, I had to hide the truck again and spend more time walking through the dark town in the middle of the night.

It was quiet, and from time to time, I

heard the hooting of an owl. There were a few lit-up windows in the townhomes on side streets despite it being fairly late at night. Were the homes' inhabitants emotionally tormented or simply unable to sleep? Or were they just up celebrating? Who knew? I shook myself mentally and concentrated on my surroundings.

As I neared the resort, I once again felt the wonderful ocean breeze. I paused in front of the hotel and looked into the distance. There was the lighthouse, our final destination. Would this light bring us sorrow or victory? Perhaps both?

CHAPTER ELEVEN

I entered the resort. The front desk was empty, and no one was in the lobby. I went up the steps quietly and did my best to make no sound entering my room so I would not awaken Thompson.

Despite being utterly drained, exhausted, and almost delirious, I sat on the edge of the bed. I tried to think clearly, but my thoughts were scrambled, like morning eggs beaten by a drunk chef. Eventually, I collapsed. That night my dreams were filled with black water all around me and dark long tentacles coming up and down out of it. Nothing else was visible. I was in the middle of the ocean, under a black sky, with the dark water absorbing me. Then all became complete blackness. I was spinning, and stars began to appear all around me. I was floating in the middle of the cosmos.

Then in the distance, I saw a dark opening, and I was terrified. I felt my body shake and sweat, but I couldn't awaken myself. Was I screaming? It was silent screams and invisible tears. Could my mind and body endure with the help of my soul?

When I finally woke up, it was a bright and beautiful morning. I stretched out my stiff legs. I seemed to be getting close to the limits of my strength and energy. I heard Thompson knock on the door. I stared at it for a while. His voice became filled with desperate concern. Poor young lad, all his hopes on an old chap like me. I finally answered him.

"Calm down, Thompson. Get us a table. I'll be right down."

His relief showed in his voice. "Thank God! I will now!"

I heard him hurry away. He was a good young man, so determined and focused. I stood up and stretched my back, walked over, and stood close to my window. It was a gorgeous morning. The rising sun shone a perfect golden color upon the water, all the way onto the sand. Seagulls were doing their usual early fly by, searching for lethargic crabs. A line of pelicans flew over. They, too, searched for food. They began circling above the water and then crashing down, trying to snatch the fish. Some were successful, and others failed over and over again. I smiled.

I got dressed, washed my face, and left the room. Thompson must have been anxiously waiting.

As I entered the dining area, I saw Thompson at our regular table next to the window. He waved to me. I noticed that there were a few more guests than usual. The season was picking up. This was good for us because the more eyes hanging around the place meant we were safer from those who were trying to cover up their movements. That meant more safety for me, the book thief.

A waiter was nowhere to be found. We sat waiting for perhaps ten minutes, and then Marco came out. He had evidently taken the place of Kit. Ritz was not in sight either. I wondered if perhaps he had sparked the wrath of Mijec and gone into hiding.

I gave Marco my order for eggs, bacon, and coffee, looked outside at the water for a moment, then, with a deep breath, I turned to Thompson.

"Young man, the last part of our journey is at hand...I have the book."

His look was incredulous. "What? Oh my God!"

"Shhhh, talk very quietly."

Immediately Thompson looked around in fear and whispered, "Sorry, sorry. Wow, you are amazing."

I smiled wryly. "The toughest part is yet to come." I leaned closer to him. "My plan is to alter the book, ruining it, essentially, but at the same time, I have to make it appear to be untouched." I smiled and sat back as Marco brought our food. Then I went on. "We must go to Boom Market and talk to Nathaniel, the owner, and ask him if he has the supplies we will need. Then I want to visit that lighthouse and case the entire area, so I know it like the back of my hand."

Thompson nodded eagerly and nervously at the same time. Then he asked, "My...my sister?"

I felt terrible that there was no news on that front. "I did not see Natalie, but I'm sure she's the one they plan to use in their ritual. Mijec will have her with him. We will trade her for the book."

A look of pure fear crossed Thompson's plain face, but it was followed by a mature, resolute expression. My admiration for the young man grew.

"Mijec will feel that he's won, but then he will see that the book is worthless. And then I'll kill him."

"What about the other cultists?"

Well, I hadn't figured that out yet. "I'm not sure. I hope something will reveal itself to us. This is our only path right now to get her back and to stop the dreamer from awakening."

Thompson nodded and applied himself to his meal.

I brought my coffee cup close to my nose.

I enjoyed the aroma while watching the slow waves roll in and break upon the shore. I tried to enjoy every moment of that breakfast, forcing my mind to be occupied with food, coffee, and the waves, blocking out the fear, anxiety, and tension, at least for a few precious moments. Thompson clearly could do no such thing. He looked sober and grim. I fervently prayed that this young man and his sister would enjoy a happy ending, but nothing in life can be guaranteed like that. Not for me, and not for him.

I finished the coffee and walked out of the resort with Thompson, feeling his nervousness carry over to me.

Boom Market was just up ahead, but on the way there, we noticed several official-looking men in uniforms asking questions of the locals. We stayed away, but I hoped it meant that Lara had gotten to her destination and given the note to Listrom. Perhaps the story of her kidnapping had sparked an investigation. I had told her to say nothing of the monster, or they'd think she was crazy. So, it was very likely that Ritz had fled town completely. I hoped they wouldn't spook Mije, but I doubted he'd leave without his precious book.

We circled around, turned the corner, and entered Boom Market. Nathaniel, the rather cheerful owner, greeted us. I asked him for several things, such as scissors, glue, tape, pencils, pens, and paints. He was very helpful, and in no time, we had a bag filled with our supplies. Now we had to head back and do the transformation of the book. No one was going to be able to use it again.

We walked through the main street, and the men we'd seen were gone. There was a young fisherman sitting on the side of the street, reading a newspaper. We suddenly heard an unpleasant and familiar yell.

"Damn readin'!"

Old Smith stood across the street from the young man. The fisherman ignored Old Smith.

"You damn readin', I say? The devils from the big city got ye brain toasted! Readin' them poison! Iducantion? Ye!"

He turned to us, looking angry.

"The sea swallow ye!! The sea swall'win' ye whole!" He turned and ran around the corner of a row of townhouses on the street. Thompson looked at me, shaking his head.

"Wow...."

"Being crazy like that is probably not a blessing," I calmly concluded, and we crossed the street to go back to the resort. It was time to reconstruct the Dark Symphony.

CHAPTER TWELVE

We tirelessly worked on our destructive craft for a couple of hours within the walls of my room as the waves hit the shore calmly and soothingly outside my open window. When our work was complete, we were both impressed. On the outside, the book still looked the same, but inside, every single page had been drastically changed in one way or another. I had a big smile on my face as I leaned against the wall next to the window and felt the ocean breeze ruffle my hair.

I had lived a life foreign to most people. Very few would consider me sane if they heard my stories. Yet, they were all true.

How does a person cope with such fantastical knowledge? How does one feel normal and calm, knowing what others don't, and facing disbelief and ridicule if it were ever brought to light? There are secrets of this world that are known to only a few. I have seen things that other people only read about in books or see on television. I have also witnessed the true power of God in my life. The energy from His true paradise has guided and protected me. I'd led an amazing life, and I am grateful for it.

As I turned my head towards the sky and the ocean, I realized that I now had very little fear of death. Nevertheless, I did not want to leave Ida and my son because of the pain it would bring them. So, again and again, I asked my Lord, my God, to see me safely through to the end of this mission. In my mind, I swore to God that this would be my final adventure, the last case.

I looked at Thompson, who I could tell was terrified but trying to be resolute. Poor, poor lad.

"Thompson, let's go see the lighthouse now."

Earlier, at the store, I read an advertisement for bicycle rentals. George Gip was the name of the man who owned the business. We went to the address, a humble white house with old walls. The porch looked like it was about to fall apart. There in a rocking chair sat a man in his sixties with long grey hair and a short grey beard. I approached him.

"Mr. Gip?"

"Ye, how you do? Got business?"

I inclined my head slightly. "Very well, thank you. We saw an ad about bicycles."

Gip squinted at me. "Ye, $2.50 each. Bring 'em back before sundown."

I handed him five dollars. He took the money and smelled it.

"Ah, good, more for my beer. There, behind th' fence."

He pointed to his left, and there behind a once-whitewashed fence, stood four old bikes. Thompson and I thanked him and took two of them. Gip was no longer looking at us; he was rocking and staring out into the distance.

"Let's go, Thompson, no time to waste."

The somewhat rusted old bicycles squeaked and were slow but nevertheless did the job. We were on our way, riding on a path above the shore. The cliffs looked magnificent. It was a beautiful place. If only I could forget the horror, the ocean hid within it!

It took us about thirty minutes riding to get to the lighthouse. We stopped and put the bikes near the steps leading down towards a wide stony path going all the way to the tall lighthouse with red and white curving stripes. We walked down, and I scanned the space around me, considering the position of the path, how many people could walk abreast, and where I would have to be to see what I needed to see. I ran through a dozen different scenarios in my head, but there was no way to predict everything for sure.

Thompson reached the lighthouse before me. "It's open, Mr. Nistage!"

"Wonderful! We will climb all the way to the top."

As I entered the gloomy lighthouse, the air felt more humid and heavy. There were only three windows to light our way. As we ascended the stairs, we disturbed a heavy layer of dust. Thompson was ahead of me, and I pulled out my handkerchief to keep from breathing the dust his hurried steps were stirring up.

Suddenly on the dark wall, I saw a vision. It was a face of a creature, horrible, contorted, indescribable. I felt a sharp pain in my chest, and terror flooded my mind. My legs shook, and I had to sit down. There was a dark power emitting from the vision. I closed my eyes, but there it was, still in front of me. I felt my body swaying side to side.

"Mr. Nistage! Mr. Nistage! Are you all right?" Thompson realized I was no longer climbing the stairs. He hurried back down, bending over me in fear. He shook my shoulder, trying to get me to open my eyes.

Thankfully, the vision faded, and I slowly snapped out of it. It must have been the Dreamer. What terror and power! I looked up at a worried Thompson. His forehead was wrinkled, and his eyes were huge and filled with concern.

I patted his arm. "I'm fine now, please

do not worry. Let's keep on going." He helped me up. "Thank you, thank you, young man," I said in what I hoped was a calm, assured voice. At my age, crazy visions were the last thing I needed during a grueling and tough climb up this very tall lighthouse.

I labored, puffed, and huffed like that foolish wolf in the fairy tale. Thompson kept slowing down to make sure I was okay. Finally, we arrived at the top and stepped out onto the catwalk surrounding the lamp. What a relief!

"It's a beautiful view, Mr. Nistage."

"It is indeed."

It was spectacular. The sun illuminated the waves as they calmly rolled towards the shore in eternal motion. Birds flew over on their never-ending quest for food. Others sat and enjoyed the sun. We could see the town, the asylum on the cliff, and the clouds appeared much closer to us. I looked down at the path leading towards the entrance of the lighthouse.

Then something caught my eye in the sky. As the sun moved to the west, the outline of an unusually large and almost full moon appeared.

I pressed my lips together and said, "It'll be tomorrow, the blood moon, our final stand, Thompson."

The young man nodded. This was going to be the last chapter of my adventures. It weighed heavily on my heart: the danger, the terror, the possibilities. I went down on my knees.

"Let's pray."

Thompson knelt next to me, clasped his hands, and closed his eyes. I took a few deep breaths, allowing the air to fully come into my body. I felt the breeze in my hair and put the palms of my hands together.

"My Father in heaven...." As I said that first line, I felt my eyes get teary. I felt a presence. "Please forgive us our sins. Make us strong, protect us from any evil that may come our way. I know I am not a perfect person. I know my mistakes have been many, but I also know your kindness and love. Fill us with your light and strength. Thank you. We say this in the name of the Holy Spirit and Jesus Christ.

Amen."

As I opened my eyes, tears slid down my cheeks. I felt a loving warmth inside my head and my hands. Thompson helped me get up slowly.

"Let's go down now, Thompson, and get to town before dark. There is one more place I'd like to visit before I sleep tonight."

He nodded, and we went back through the door. Going down was, of course, not as bad as climbing up, and in a much shorter period of time, we were on our bikes and heading back towards the ailing town.

I had seen a poster saying that the jazz singer Pammi would be performing at Café Chalie that night. I don't know why, but I felt the need to go and listen and immerse myself in the music I had loved for forty years.

We got back to Gip's place and parked our bikes against the neglected fence. He was nowhere to be seen, but we'd kept our part of the bargain. By the time we got back to the resort, it was fully dark. I left Thompson in his room and headed to the café to hear one last jazz song —perhaps the one last jazz song of my life.

The moon hung high as I faced the door of Café Chalie. Inside, the lights were dim, just as the last time, and only a few tables were taken. I sat down but only ordered juice and a pastry. Pammi was already on the tiny stage in the corner. Her band consisted of only one man with a saxophone and another at a small piano. Pammi smiled and greeted everyone, then the music began to play, and her soft, smooth voice flowed together with it.

"In the thin air,
A lonely feather floats,
And with his eyes,
He watches it slowly fall,

"And the whiskey
Never tasted so dull,
For a moment,
He forgot even his name,

"The street lamp broken,

The wind unspoken,
You forgot your name,
Never like this before,
Whiskey glass no more.

"Fill it up,
Fill it up.
No more memories please,
He must forget,
To live without regret,
But he can't remember,
Where the pain came from,
And if it's still there,
How can he go home?

"He should remember,
The last time he laughed.
That memory will stir him,
Bring him back home.

"Ohhhh, once that smile shone,
The laugh like a roar,
A happy, happy lion,
Stood there no more.

"A shell and illusion,
What's left there, inside?
Pain and confusion,
That drink won't provide.

"Oh, decide, oh decide,
Think back, think truth,
Think love, think good,
Think God, think, think, think…

"Perhaps it's not too late,
To put away the glass,
Open your eyes.
There's so much to life,
So much to find out, so much to guess,

"Put away the glass,
Oh poor stranger, put away that glass,
Your eyes tell a story,
One I don't need to guess.

"Farewell,
Farewell."

As the song finished, I sure was glad I wasn't drinking alcohol. That was it for me, as I needed all the strength I could get. I left the place and safely made it to my room. I sat by the window and looked out at the moon for a while. Then I prayed and got in bed, hoping to have no nightmares.

Yet, at night he came again. The dreamer, his eyes closed, yet his mind so sharp, cutting deep into my subconscious, letting me know of the pain that would await the world if I failed in my mission. How had it come to this? An old man like me, holding the keys to the world's salvation? Perhaps that was my own pride coming through in the dream. The book was ruined, and the deed was already done. It was the girl's life that mattered now.

But the nightmares went on. The long hallway of darkness inside the deep, dreamy waters tormented me, shook me, and made me unstable. I screamed, but it was silent. I cried, but my face was dry. The horror, the fear, and some of the deepest human emotions touched the nerves of my whole being. How much could one man take?

CHAPTER THIRTEEN

I woke up in a cold sweat, and it was still dark. I propped myself against the wall and sat there staring at the night ocean. I could barely see the waves; only the strip of water illuminated by the moon was clearly visible. I knew some of the ocean's secrets. Perhaps I wished I didn't, but would I still be who I was then? Luc Nistage was the sum of all his experiences, even the supernatural ones. I could not change that. If it was God's will, I could handle it. Let the morning come. The blood moon was upon us.

I must have slept again.

There it was, the beautiful rays of the morning sun. Again the painful thought jumped into my mind about this possibly being the last morning of my life, so I'd better enjoy this view. *No. I will make it.* I turned my face away from the window as I sat up. *I will eat breakfast as usual. Then I will take it easy, rest most of the day, and get ready for the night at the lighthouse.*

I met Thompson in the hallway, and we went down to eat. Neither of us was talkative; our nervousness seemed to make the air around us vibrate. From time to time, my heart beat faster, and I took deep breaths and tried to eat my food calmly.

We rested and sunned ourselves outside the resort, and later in the afternoon, we walked to where I had hidden Kit's old truck. Before dinnertime, we drove to the lighthouse in order to hide inside before the cultists got there.

My reconnaissance of the day before had identified a good place to hide the vehicle close to the road but out of sight if the cultists came from the same direction I had observed before. I hated for it to be as far away as it was because if we had to run for it, we would be exposed to the cultists for a good period, and I didn't know if they carried guns. But it was the best situation I could create under the circumstances.

We made our way down the rocky path towards the lighthouse and went in. Once again, I had to labor all the way up the twisting staircase, but this time it actually felt easier. We sat at the top, watching the waves and the path, waiting patiently. It came before we knew it, and so did the giant blood moon, which hung like a giant pendant over the dark ocean.

As the night progressed, we finally heard a commotion coming from the tree line. As the cult members got closer, we could tell they were chanting. Then my heart began to pound as the cultists emerged from the trees.

Thompson gasped, and his hands trembled as he finally saw his sister, with her hands tied, dressed all in white, being led by Mijec, with his bald head exposed, wearing a black robe. All the others wore black robes and hoods.

Mijec stopped in the middle of the rocky path and pushed Natalie to her knees. All the cultists fell to their knees as well. As Mijec began to yell a chant, they all seemed to enter a mindless trance, swaying slowly with their heads down, except for Natalie. She was in tears, begging for mercy. Her face was filled with desperation and terror.

"Ag guhhat dathagget, ignzh ar infahgg, a aggtthog! Idesggaht Idesggaht!"

Mijec looked up at the lighthouse. I could see his black eyes even from afar. I gripped my revolver. Mijec screamed directly at us.

"I know you're there! I knew you'd come! You want to trade, yes? My book for the girl?"

I stood slowly and held up the book. I could see the other cultists still seemed to be in their trance. This was good. However, Mijec had a knife on his belt, and I had to be very careful. He could kill Natalie if I shot and missed, so I had to fake the trade first.

"Natalie! Are you all right?" Thompson yelled.

"Yes! Thompson! Help me!" she shouted back.

"Mijec, we are coming down with the book," I called down at him.

Thompson and I looked at each other. In the time it took for us to get down the stairs, Mijec could kill Natalie, but that was the chance we had to take. We hurried down the steps as quickly as we could. As we drew closer to the door, Thompson went first in case Mijec tried to attack us, but as the door opened, we could see that he was in the same spot, holding his knife in his left hand.

"He is coming...," Mijec screeched maniacally and pushed Natalie towards us, holding onto her by the shoulder. Throw the book, and she can run to you!"

I couldn't trust him, but what else could I do? "Let go of her first," I said roughly, and thank God, he did. I threw the book, and as he caught it, Natalie embraced Thompson. "Go," I said to them in a low voice. They edged toward the path.

Mijec began to laugh, a high-pitched, insane sound. "He is coming! And now his master will be awakened too!" He flipped open the book, and his black eyes grew very large in astonishment, quickly changing to rage. He raised his knife, screaming, "You demons! You destroyed the precious texts!"

As he charged at us, I shot him in the chest, and when he slowed down and swayed, I delivered the final bullet right into his evil skull. He fell, face forward, and blood poured out unto the rocks.

Suddenly the ground began to shake, and waves started smashing the rocks around us, growing bigger and bigger. I turned around. Behind the lighthouse, among the waves, the tall figure with six tentacles and long human arms emerged. Thompson had already untied Natalie's hands as I turned to them.

"We must run now! He is coming!"

Even being my age, the adrenaline and terror propelled me as I ran ahead, with Natalie behind me, followed by clumsy Thompson. As Natalie and I got up to higher ground and turned, we suddenly realized that Thompson was not with us. He was lower on the path, trying to stand up. He had tripped and fallen and evidently twisted his ankle.

The path began to collapse, and the

lighthouse shook. The bright eyes of the monster appeared among the waves near Thompson with the blood moon behind them. His tentacles wrapped around Thompson's legs, and as the lighthouse collapsed into the ocean, the monster dragged Thompson into the water with him. Natalie screamed and screamed, and I had to hang onto her as she tried to run towards the water, but it was too late. Mijec, the cultists, and even the shoreline had disappeared into the dark water. I had to drag her away and force her into the truck.

Natalie cried loudly, deeply, and sorrowfully; she trembled, and so did I, but at least I had saved her — perhaps I had saved the world as well. And Thompson had done his part.

***

A week later...

I sat by the window in my cozy home, watching the street from above, drinking my favorite black tea. Beside me sat my wife Ida, doing the same thing. The city was full of life.

At the end of it all, my God, my Lord,

had gotten me through.

Alexander Semenyuk (also known as Oleksandr Semenyuk) is a Ukrainian-American author. He was born in Lutsk, Ukraine, in 1986. At 14, he immigrated to the United States. Alexander's favorite genres are sci-fi, horror and fantasy. Early in life, Alexander was greatly influenced by classic literature and, since childhood, dreamed of becoming a writer.

www.ingramcontent.com/pod-product-compliance
Lightning Source LLC
Chambersburg PA
CBHW020133180626
46810CB00004B/1541